THE SOUTH COAST

AN EDDIE HOLLAND NOVEL

JOHN H. MATTHEWS

This is a work of fiction. Names, characters, places, and incidents either are the product of the author's imagination or are used fictitiously, and any resemblance to actual persons, living or dead, business establishments, events or locales is entirely coincidental.

The South Coast
Written by John H. Matthews

First Edition 2013
Second Edition 2015
ISBN: 978-0-9897233-3-6

Bluebullseye Press
www.bluebullseyepress.com
A division of Bluebullseye LLC

Editorial services provided by Cogberry Productions

*To Dad for filling the
shelves with books.*

*To Brennan for pulling all
the books off the shelves.*

CHAPTER 1

The man fell to his knees in the warm surf of the Gulf of Mexico. The salt water struck his skin abruptly, momentarily easing the pain. His thoughts were not of his wife or his children, and his life did not flash before his eyes. He thought of the last face he had seen and how little expression it showed. He thought of the sound of the gun and the few moments that he thought he hadn't been hit, that the bullet had missed its target.

As the rush of blood from the hole in his stomach drained him, he collapsed into the water.

CHAPTER 2

Eddie Holland woke up in his bed, a rare occurrence the last six months considering his habit of late nights falling asleep in front of the TV. Staring at the ceiling, he weighed the pros and cons of getting up. No pros came to mind.

Rolling over he glanced at the clock and saw that it was already ten o'clock. He groaned as he swung his legs over the edge of the bed and stood up. He pulled on a pair of shorts over the underwear he'd slept in and a pair of socks from the floor that passed the smell test then tied his blue and silver Brooks running shoes. He pulled the door to his apartment closed and left it unlocked so he didn't have to carry his keys. Once he got to the sidewalk he moved easily from a walk to a jog and then to a run and was quickly up to his pace as his heart beat out the time.

The sun struck his skin and he felt the dryness in the air that most of Texas had been feeling for more than a month. The drought was into its fifth week and the already dry earth was cracked and starved. The soil drank in Eddie's sweat as it collided with the ground.

Back through his front door an hour later, he started his shower and stepped in before the water had warmed up.

Mostly clean and halfway refreshed, he opened his closet and stared at the row of dark suits hung neatly on wire hangers and wrapped in clear plastic, just as the dry cleaner had left them half a year earlier. He reached past the suits and grabbed a pair of jeans from the shelf above them and a Texas women's roller derby T-shirt from the clean clothes in his laundry basket.

On his way to the front door, Eddie stopped and looked at the dozen or so hats lined up on the bookshelf in his living room and finally selected the straw duckbill he'd bought in Wicker Park while working out of the field office in Chicago.

He turned and looked in the mirror beside the front door while putting the hat on, and then he really looked at himself. The dark circles that had been under his eyes for years were gone, and he had color to his skin again. The T-shirt fit snug over his taut 165 pounds. The weight he had put on was gone and the suits in his closet would likely hang off of him now.

He walked out the front door of his apartment, down the stairs, through the courtyard lined with sad brown grass and a lone cactus, perhaps the only life enjoying the weather, and stopped at the pay phone outside the manager's office. Putting a quarter in, he dialed, it rang, and a woman's voice came from the other end.

"When the hell are you going to get a cell phone like the rest of the civilized world?"

"Good god, do you always answer your phone like that?" he replied.

"Only when caller ID tells me it's a payphone calling and the only jackass on the face of the earth who still uses a payphone is my brother."

"Coffee?" he asked.

"Of course I want coffee. Meet me downstairs in fifteen," she hung up.

EDDIE LEANED ON the glass front of Shelley's office

building in downtown Austin. She came out the front door of the building to his left and flicked her freshly lit cigarette to the sidewalk and stepped on it.

"Most people wait until they're outside then light up nowadays."

"I just like pissing off the rent-a-cop they keep in the lobby," she said.

He shook his head. "Mother Theresa had nothing on you."

"What can I say, I'm an anti-social smoker."

They walked across the street to a café, sat at a table in the window with a view of the street, and the waitress brought them a pot of coffee. He watched his sister add cream, stir it in, and take her first sip before speaking, knowing how she thrives on the ritual.

"So, got anything for me?"

"Shit, really? You go right to that? No 'how you been', or 'how's the kids'?"

"When did you get so touchy?" he said. "How are you? How are the kids?"

"Too late and yes, I think I have something for you. One of our corporate clients comes by, an old college friend of one of our senior partners. After they met the partner comes to me, tells me it's a complete hush-hush, off the books job."

"That doesn't sound like usual business practice for your firm, they have the best reputation in town," Eddie said.

"Very true, but these guys go way back, both fraternity legacies at UT for undergrad, went on to Harvard Law together. Probably more than a couple skeletons between them."

"Some of those fraternities are closer than real family."

"You got it," Shelley said. "So he has this thing that needs done but doesn't want anyone else at the practice to know about it and doesn't want the police involved at all."

"So you run right out and tell an FBI agent? Remind me not to trust you with any secrets."

"I have several guys I go to for jobs, but none like this. Not only do I need complete discretion but I need to watch out for the firm, too. I figure if I get you to handle it and there's anything less than kosher, it can get passed on to the proper people. Anyway you got fired from the FBI."

"I'm on a leave of absence," Eddie said. "I didn't get fired. I can go back whenever I'm ready."

Shelley leaned back and looked at her brother and sipped her coffee.

"Still not feeling it?" she asked.

"Nope," Eddie said. "Right now I'm enjoying myself for the first time in five years. I'm relaxing, running a lot, and get to see my big sister more often."

"Think you'll ever go back?" Shelley said.

"Probably. I'm good at it," he said. "But for now it's all about me."

They sat in silence together and drank their coffee.

"You gone to see Dad lately?"

Eddie looked at his coffee, deciding whether to ignore his sister's question.

"Nah," Eddie said. "Been pretty busy."

"He'd enjoy seeing you," she said.

"That's what they say," Eddie said. "It's just… it's hard."

"Nobody said it wasn't, but he's still our Dad in there."

"So what's this mystery case?" Eddie changed the subject.

"Missing person."

"Missing person, and they don't want the cops involved?"

"This guy, he's the CEO of a tech company that does only government contracts. Real high-level spooky shit.

He's worried about any information getting out that could hurt them."

"Who's missing?"

"A guy that's worked there a few years, head of their network security. He hasn't been heard from in about a month, nobody answers his phone or his door. This has to be off the radar, completely quiet. Simply find this guy and get him back to the CEO."

"I understand."

"Do you? This means no Gus. Completely on your own."

"Got it."

Once the pot was empty Shelley reached into her oversized purse and pulled out a manila envelope and put it on the table. She leaned over and hugged Eddie for longer than she realized then walked back across the street, causing a delivery truck driver to slam on his brakes and honk at her. She stopped and stared at the driver then continued into her building.

CHAPTER 3

FIVE YEARS AGO

The black Ford Explorer traveled down M Street in Georgetown then turned left onto Key Bridge to exit Washington, D.C., as the ice began to fall.

"Shit," Eddie said to himself. "Nothing worse than Northern Virginia drivers in bad weather."

It was 8:40 a.m. as he maneuvered through traffic on Highway 66 through Arlington. Traffic was heavy and Eddie didn't have any patience. He reached down and pressed a glowing blue button and the white and blue lights began flashing from inside the grill of the large

SUV and from the back window. He moved left onto the shoulder and passed groups of cars that were already slowing down due to the small amount of precipitation.

Ten minutes later he exited onto Chain Bridge Road then took a left onto Lewinsville Road. He turned onto the private drive for the large building that contains the National Counterterrorism Center. At the gated checkpoint, he provided his FBI credentials and continued to the parking lot.

Inside the front door, Eddie removed his pistol from its holster and handed it to the security guard, who cleared the weapon as Eddie moved through the metal detector, then retrieved his gun and took the elevator to the fourth floor of the south wing where the FBI housed their branch of the Joint Terrorism Task Force.

"Eddie, where've you been?" an older man in a black suit said.

"Sorry, Ben, you know Fairfax traffic," Eddie said.

"You're just in time," Ben said. "We're about to get the stream."

"Where the hell did this come from?" Eddie said. "When I left at 9:30 last night there was nothing on the board for today."

"This is coming straight from Langley," Ben said. "They say they have good intel and need to act on it fast."

"And we find out when wheels are already off the ground?" Eddie said. "They sure don't understand the 'joint' part of Joint Terrorism Task Force."

"CIA says it's their op, their intel, and they say it's good," Ben said.

Eddie walked with the lead FBI agent into an interior room with no windows and a solid steel door. Once the door was closed the lights dimmed and one wall of the room became a television screen showing detailed video from a drone flying over the desert of Afghanistan.

Glancing around the small room he saw the three other FBI agents assigned to this task force, as well as four men and one woman from the CIA who took up the back row of chairs. A man from the agency who went only by the name Sanders stood and walked to the front of the room.

"I should've known it was him," Eddie turned to Ben. "This guy cares more about racking up body counts than actually targeting Al Qaeda."

"OK, ladies and gentleman," Sanders said. "We are taking action on a clandestine cell in the desert approximately 40 miles from Kandahar. Intel suggests at least 10 men, as many women, and 18 children."

"Have we had eyes on the ground confirming?" Ben said.

"The village is remote and unapproachable from any direction without being spotted and targeted," Sanders said. "We have what we believe to be proof from our satellite and drone reconnaissance that the residents of this village are assembling suicide vests for use either in country or to be brought to the United States."

"What's today's operation?" Eddie said.

"We will be entering the village, gauging the threat, then eliminating any threat if present," Sanders said.

"When you say 'we'," Eddie said, "I'm assuming you don't mean yourself, I mean, that would be a bit too dirty for you, wouldn't it?"

"Eddie," Special Agent in Charge Ben Olsen said, "Play nice."

The CIA officer stared at Eddie then continued.

"We are supported on the ground by the U.S. Army Rangers, 2nd Battalion," Sanders said. "They are currently en route. They dropped from 34,000 feet in a high altitude, high opening drop to maintain silence, about four clicks from the village. We should be receiving first transmission from them any time."

"What about extraction?" Ben said.

"Two Blackhawk helicopters are on the deck five minutes outside the village to extract our soldiers and any assets they are able to collect," Sanders said.

The monitor continued to show the aerial view of the village as the rooms occupants spoke softly to each other, each agency careful not to let anyone from another hear them. The heat-sensing camera of the drone showed the subtle movement of the soldiers on the ground as they approached the five-building village.

"We have a visual on the village and are approaching now," a large voice came over the speakers in the room. "Two minutes until contact."

The display in front of them changed as the Rangers began broadcasting their location information from transceivers in their vests to the drone above, which bounced off a satellite then updated the monitor in the room. Twenty small red squares appeared beside the moving images on screen, each representing one of the troops on the ground in Afghanistan, with the last name of each Ranger following their bobbing identifier.

"We are at the village and beginning assessment," the red dot with the name 'Akins' following it lit up as the large voice again came across the speakers.

The men and women in the room stared at the display, safe in their secure room in Virginia while these 20 men moved through a remote and possibly hostile village in the desert of Afghanistan on the other side of the planet.

"Alpha team is at the target and putting eyes in place," Akins said from the desert.

A moment later a smaller screen beside the large one came on showing the stream from a tiny infrared camera one of the Rangers had been able to slip through the wooden slat of a window in the building the CIA suspected might be making suicide vests.

"You should have visuals now," Akins said.

"Confirmed," Sanders said.

The image from the small camera was noticeably blurrier than the aerial view of the desert and the room appeared red and glowing from the infrared signal. As the Ranger moved the camera all of the occupants of the room in Virginia stared to decipher the images coming across to them.

"This appears to be one long table," Sanders said, as he used a laser pointer on the monitor. "It looks like an assembly line, these are the vests, and here are the explosives waiting to be sewn into them."

"Or it's where they make their clothes," Eddie said. "Unless they run out to Abercrombie when they need new outfits."

Ben jabbed Eddie in the ribs with his elbow.

The CIA man looked to the back of the room at his other officers and each nodded slightly in confirmation of their boss's determination.

"Alpha team," Sanders said into the microphone. "We have confirmation. Proceed with the operation."

"Understood," Akins said.

Single word orders came from the Army leader on the ground, alerting his men to the status of their operation and the red dots on the screen began to move more quickly. They broke into four groups of five on the screen in front of them and each group approached one of the buildings they had studied from satellite images for the last two weeks.

The teams entered their designated buildings at the same time and sounds came from the leader of each team over the speakers in the room.

"Bravo team is clear," a voice came from the building at the top of the screen. "No one home."

"Charlie team is clear."

"Delta team is clear."

One by one each building was determined to be empty.

"Where are the villagers?" Eddie said. "This doesn't feel right."

The Rangers began to move through the village, entering and exiting the remaining buildings while others covered them and stood guard, their weapons always up and at the ready. They pulled books and mobile phones and dumped them into plastic trash bags.

Alpha team moved to the factory and one of the remaining team members breached the door and entered.

"Clear," the Ranger said.

Akins entered the factory and pulled the flashlight from his belt and turned it on, shining it on the items lining the long table and his stomach tightened.

"We have nothing," Akins said.

"Clarify," Sanders said.

"The factory appears to be making nothing but clothing," Akins said.

The room in Virginia was silent.

"Clear the whole building, don't leave anything unturned," Sanders said.

A young Ranger opened a wooden chest on the floor at one end of the room and heard the distinctive click of a pin being released from a Claymore mine. He froze, staring at the chest and hoped what he heard wasn't what he knew it was and reached up to clutch the photo of his 4 year old daughter taped to his helmet.

The Ranger was killed instantly, cut in two by the direct blast. Shrapnel embedded in the neck of another Ranger and the flow of blood from the wound increased quickly. Akins took a direct hit in the leg and fell to the floor.

Delta team entered the building.

"We have one down, one injured," the lead Delta team soldier said. "And Captain Akins is down. We need medical support immediately."

A Blackhawk helicopter landed behind the factory building and two Army medics in full combat gear came into the room. One worked to stabilize the Ranger hit in the neck, only to have him bleed out before the flow of blood could be stopped. The other medic put pressure on Akins femoral artery to reduce the bleeding from the piece of skin and stump where his right leg used to be.

CHAPTER 4

Eddie sat under a large oak tree in his 1969 VW Karmann Ghia convertible he'd owned since high school. Parked a few doors down from the missing man's house, he read through the file his sister had given him. He had long ago replaced the original AM/FM unit in the car with a CD player, which was turned on low with Guy Clark singing stories of Texas and lost love.

Peter Miller is 31 years old. Born and raised in Dallas, he went to college at the University of Texas in Austin and graduated in the top of his class in computer science. He's single and lives alone in the rented house and is employed by a government contracting company called BaseCamp Technology. His parents live in Dallas and are the beneficiaries of his life insurance and 401K if anything happens to him.

Finding no enlightenment in the pages of the folder, he leaned back on the headrest and stared at the house. The bungalow wasn't the worst looking one on the street, but wasn't the best either. A few missing tiles on the roof, faded paint and the yard was overgrown. After 20 minutes and no activity, Eddie turned the stereo off and got out of the car.

"Time to play detective," he said out loud to himself.

He walked across the street, through Peter Miller's yard and to the back door of the clapboard bungalow. The sun had moved down in the sky and the back of the house was covered in shadows from the shade trees surrounding the back yard.

He knocked on the back door loud enough to wake anyone inside and waited. A minute later he repeated the knock and cupped his hands around his eyes to peer through the dirty glass into the kitchen.

Eddie pulled a tattered, brown work glove from the back pocket of his jeans and put it on his right hand. Gripping the doorknob with his gloved hand, he pulled the carpenter's chisel from his other pocket and shoved it into doorjamb. With an efficient heave against the door, the 1920s wood creaked and popped before giving in. He stepped inside, closing the door behind him, and stood in the back of the kitchen for several minutes to listen to the house.

This was his favorite part, what made him do what he does: Being alone in a stranger's home and looking at their life to understand them. He'd learned to do it at just the right time of the evening while enough light is still coming in through the windows. Too bright, and you risk only looking in the obvious places. Too dark, and you just can't see anything. Using a flashlight only blinds you to the rest of the room. Your eyes adjust to the brightness and you can't see past the light.

Once the house was still again and his eyes had grown accustomed to the low light, he moved through the room. Using his gloved hand, he touched things as he thought Peter Miller would. Looking at the teapot on the stove, he reached up and opened the cabinet on the right to see a dozen mismatched coffee cups, each with a different company logo on it. He could feel the path used to move through the kitchen and to the archway into the living room.

Without looking, he reached to the wall on his right and his hand landed on the light switch, held there a moment, then came back to his side with the lights still off.

He moved to the closest seat in the living room, the left end of the sofa, and sat down. His body rested into the impression left behind from night after night of the same action of the home's resident. Looking to the left he saw the sidebar, with bottles of different brands of Irish whiskey in varying states of emptiness and a mostly full bottle of amaretto off to the side.

He ran his right hand across the surface of the center cushion beside him, his fingers sensing an indentation from someone sitting there. On the floor to the right of his feet was a crumpled up afghan that looked like it had been covering somebody's feet.

Peter Miller has a girlfriend, he thought, looking back at the amaretto then again to the afghan on the floor.

Pleased with himself for his detective work, he got up and moved to the built-in holding a flat screen TV, a row of DVDs and a several shelves of books. The DVDs were standard issue 30-something tech guy titles: *Pulp Fiction*, *The Godfather*, *North by Northwest*, the *Star Wars* trilogy and every season of *The Simpsons* and *Family Guy*. Lying on top of the Blu-ray player were *Philadelphia Story* and *Sleepless in Seattle*, further confirming the presence of a woman in Peter Miller's life. Whether they were brought over to make him watch or he had placed them here to make her think he has a sensitive side, Eddie hadn't detected yet.

Moving on to the books, there was a mix of classic titles and modern best sellers. Seeing *The Grapes of Wrath* side-by-side with *Atlas Shrugged* made Eddie pause at the thought of the polar opposite ideologies being forced to coexist in such close proximity. An image of Ayn Rand and John Steinbeck slugging it out flashed through his mind, but the conclusion of that bout would have to be pondered later.

A row of travel books took up the bottom shelf. Prague, Budapest, and Vienna filled the post-college Travel 101 category. An assortment of titles about Machu Picchu, South Africa, and hiking the Appalachian Trail fit the "turning 30 and wanting to do something with my life" genre. All of the travel books spines smooth from lack of use, a sign of trips never taken. Past those were some local guides on San Antonio and Austin that had seen some use. Eddie pulled out one with the most worn cover and started flipping through it.

Inside the back cover was a foldout map of south Texas. Notes written in pencil on the edges gave distances from Austin to Corpus Christi, Padre Island,

Brownsville and the bridge over the Rio Grande to Matamoros, Mexico.

Taking the book with him, Eddie stood and walked back through the living room to the kitchen. The light from the windows was almost gone.

Eddie pulled the door shut behind him and retreated back across the street to his car and drove away with the lights off, pulling the knob to turn them on only as he turned the corner from 13th onto Salina then made a couple more turns through the neighborhood to make sure nobody was following him. Once satisfied he headed down to Cesar Chavez then west to catch the Congress Avenue Bridge south to go home.

CHAPTER 5

The next morning Eddie was up and out for an early run. Early in Austin would usually mean it was already 90 degrees, but in the drought it was already in triple digits. He ran with no shirt as always. Sweat covered his skin in the heat and glaring sun.

Going over in his head what he had learned the day before, he contemplated if he had enough to call Shelley but knew he didn't. After getting home and stopping to do a hundred push-ups on the walkway to his apartment, he showered, dressed, and selected his chocolate brown pinstriped flat cap. He then drove downtown, past the convention center, and pulled up to a diner and parked next to a black Dodge Charger with several antennas on the back window.

He walked into the diner and with a few quick steps to the counter he slapped a man on the back as he was taking a big drink of coffee.

"Jesus Christ, Eddie! Can't you just call me like normal person?" the man said.

"Where's the fun in that, Gus. Anyway, I wanted to make sure you weren't sleeping on the job and wasting my hard earned tax money," Eddie said.

"I have a gun and I will shoot you," Gus said.

Eddie motioned to the waitress for a cup of coffee then turned back to Gus.

Gus Ramirez was Eddie's oldest friend. They went to high school together, then college and graduate school, both of them receiving their degrees in criminology. Then they applied for the FBI, were accepted, and went to Quantico for their training. After that they were separated for the first time when Gus was assigned to St. Louis and Eddie went to the field office in D.C.

"I need a favor," Eddie said. He reached into his jeans pocket and handed Gus a piece of paper with Peter Miller's name, social security number and address. "I need to know if this guy has any record and what he drives."

"Anything else?" Gus glared at Eddie over his coffee cup.

"Nah, that should do it."

"You do know I'm not a beat cop who speed guns high school kids for easy tickets, right? I'm an FBI agent."

"I know, I know, Agent Ramirez. But if you call in a request for information, it doesn't get logged or tracked by the locals and I keep off their radar."

"Oh, because you're still working as a private dick without a license and don't want to get caught?" Gus said.

"Something like that," Eddie said. "But more because after twenty years of being friends we know way too much about each other to not help when asked."

"So, what's this one?" Gus said while he read the piece of paper. "Another cheating husband?"

"Nope. Got myself a bona fide missing persons case."

"And what are you supposed to do?" Gus asked.

"I guess make him not missing," Eddie said.

"And you've talked to local PD?"

"This is a black op, no PD, no FBI. Not even supposed to be talking to you."

"You're not a very good private detective, you know that, don't you?"

"Never claimed to be," Eddie said.

"I'll check the guy out, and let you know," Gus said. "Still no phone?"

Eddie shook his head. "Still no phone. I'd usually have you leave a message with Shelley, but she can't know you're helping. I'll just get a hold of you later."

FOR LUNCH EDDIE sat on a bench overlooking Town Lake and ate a burger he'd picked up at P. Terry's Burger Stand on South Lamar. He flipped through the travel guide taken from Peter Miller's home, going page by page, looking to see which might be more worn than the ones before or after it.

Turning a page, he saw the faded crease of an earmark fold in the corner. Moving his eyes over to the heading it said New Braunfels, Texas. The rest of the text held nothing illuminating. The town had German heritage. There's a water park and a limestone quarry. Nothing said 'Peter Miller Is Here'.

Eddie looked up from the book and out across the lake to the downtown skyline. A rowboat moved through the water. Going back to the book, he opened the back cover and unfolded the map with the pencil marks. He scanned down Interstate 35 from Austin to

New Braunfels. At first glance there was nothing, just the small city area and a lot of open farmland.

He was just about to flip back to the book when a small mark caught his eye. Holding the map up in front of him at an angle to let the sunlight catch it just right, there was a very small circle that had been drawn on the map just east of the city then lightly erased. Only a slight discoloration remained but holding the paper up close the ridge of the pencil mark was barely visible, where the circle had been showed nothing of interest.

An hour later, Eddie was driving down Interstate 35 to make the 50-mile drive to New Braunfels, the travel guide's map open on the seat beside him. The CD player churned out the gravelly voice of Townes Van Zandt and Emmylou Harris singing 'If I Needed You' and Eddie sang along, off-key.

Eddie exited I-35 as close as he could tell would get him to the erased location on the map. Heading east off the highway he drove slowly, thinking that might make it easier to spot a clue. For several miles, none showed up.

He wound around on the roads lined by farmland, making decisions on which way to go at each T junction, based on the tiny map. As he drove down one straight stretch he reached and turned the stereo off and listened out the window as a buzzing sound got louder. A single engine plane flew across the road in front of him only a couple dozen feet off the ground, the wings waving sloppily back and forth.

"I'll mark that down as a clue," Eddie said out loud then turned the direction the plane was headed.

A quarter mile down the next road was a municipal airport with a single runway and a couple of hangars. A sign at the road informed him that private lessons were available. As best as Eddie could tell, he was in the middle of the circle on the map.

Following the signs, he pulled up in front of the business offering lessons, parked the car and walked up to the hangar where an older looking man was working with an engine part on a workbench.

"You the instructor?" Eddie asked. The man turned towards him and looked over his bifocals then back to the engine part.

"I'm the instructor, the receptionist, the mechanic, the accountant, and the janitor," the man said.

"If you're the instructor, then who's in the plane?" Eddie asked as he watched down the runway at the small plane he'd seen, which was now taxiing towards the hanger.

"That one's a rental. Students who've gotten their licenses come and rent it to get more hours."

Eddie watched a middle-aged man with a round belly and aviator glasses that were way too large for his face climb out of the cockpit and grab his bag and camera from the passenger's seat. The man tossed the keys to the instructor and said he'd see him next week and walked off to a pickup parked beside the hanger. Eddie turned his attention back to the instructor.

"I was wondering if you could help me out. I'm looking for a man named Peter Miller, might have been down here from Austin."

"Not only do I know him, but he's supposed to be taking his first solo flight right now, but hasn't shown up for the last few lessons," the man sat the engine part down and wiped each finger off with a rag that was dirtier than his hands.

"Strange thing is he's paid up through the end of the course. Not like a person to just quit when they're so close to getting their license."

Eddie thought of the travel guides from Peter Miller's house and the scribbled pencil distances to south Texas and Mexico.

"He ever mention anything about flying to Matamoros, Mexico?"

"He never said anything about Matamoros specifically, but I do recall him asking early on if there were any rules or protocols about flying over the border, due to customs and the like."

"What did you tell him?"

"There's plenty of rules; it's still a foreign country. To fly across any border, you have to be on a filed flight plan. There's an aviation border called the Air Defense Identification Zone, or ADIZ. Before you cross that zone you have to alert air traffic control. Once you cross over into Mexico you have to land at the closest airport to clear customs."

"So you definitely can't just fly into Mexico undetected."

"Not easily," the man continued with a sly grin.

Eddie looked out at the tarmac, imagined Peter Miller taking off in the single engine Cessna, and then turned back to the man.

"Thanks for your help. If you think of anything else or hear from Peter, would you leave me a message at this number?" Eddie handed him a card with his name and Shelley's phone number.

"Sure thing," the man said as Eddie headed back out to his car, the interstate, and eventually, home.

CHAPTER 6

Shelley came out of the building and over to the café where Eddie was already into his second cup of coffee. He poured her a cup and she started her mixing.

"Peter Miller has a girlfriend and has been taking flying lessons from a municipal airport in New Braunfels," Eddie paused to sip his coffee. "He also has some interest or connection with Mexico, possibly Matamoros specifically."

"Not bad for two days, baby brother," Shelley said. "You talk to the girlfriend?"

"That's next. Don't even know who she is yet. I figured she's either with him or has no idea where he is, so I followed another trail first."

"How are you going to find her?"

"Quality detecting," he said.

THREE DAYS INTO the case and Eddie was back where he started, sitting under the same oak tree just down from Peter Miller's bungalow east of downtown. A late night drive past the house the night before resulted in a passenger seat full of mail from the box at the curb. Eddie looked through it while keeping an eye on the house and the street in front and behind him in the rearview mirror.

Among the junk mail flyers for grocery stores and envelopes full of coupons were bills for car insurance, cable and a cell phone. Eddie tore open the cell phone bill and started scanning the numbers that had been dialed and numbers that had called Peter Miller's phone, looking for duplicates that might be the girlfriend. A glance at the rearview mirror showed a car coming up the street. Eddie looked back down like he was reading the bill and watched the car go by him out of the corner of his eye, a woman in Lexus convertible talking on her cell phone.

A few numbers started repeating on the phone bill and Eddie underlined them with a pen. Then he noticed a call from a pay phone in Round Rock, Texas, about half an hour north of Austin. Going back through the pages he found three more from the same phone number on that month's bill. Checking the dates on the insurance company calendar in his glove box, each call was made on a Sunday morning and lasted only twenty seconds.

After several hours of surveillance on the house, Eddie pulled out of his space at the curb and followed his ritual through the neighborhood to watch for followers. Driving downtown to a 7-11 he went in and bought a coffee and got a handful of quarters changed from dollar bills. Going out to the pay phone at the sidewalk he opened the cell phone bill and started dialing underlined phone numbers.

The first number gave him the weekend answering service for a Dr. Newman. By the calming tone of the woman answering he decided Dr. Newman was a psychiatrist and marked through the number on the bill.

The second number was the pay phone in Round Rock and it rang a dozen times without anyone picking up. Eddie hung up and put a question mark beside the number to go back to if the other two numbers didn't pay off. As he looked for the next number to dial, the phone rang in front of his face. He jumped back and stared at it, then looked around to see if some local drug dealer used this phone as a contact point, but nobody was near. He picked up the handset and put it to his ear.

"Hello," he said in a gruff voice, trying to alter his own voice but coming off more like a guy trying to change his voice.

"Who is this?" asked a gruff voice from the other end that was actually gruff and not just pretending to be.

"You called me. Who's this?" Eddie tried to stall.

"Listen to me, you piece of shit. You called me. It rang twelve times, and you hung up," the man sounded somewhere between agitated and pissed off, with a hint of 'I can kick your ass' thrown in for good measure. There was the trace of an accent that Eddie couldn't quite identify.

Eddie cursed caller ID to himself and went for broke.

"This is Peter Miller," he said. Nothing but silence came from the other end for a full ten count before a click came across the line and the phone went dead.

Eddie paused, took a few deep breaths, and then again dialed the number that had generated the return call. Instead of ringing on the other end of the line all he heard was the distinctive 'this phone is out of order' message blaring back at him through the earpiece.

Eddie stared at the pay phone then looked around and back at the phone. He pulled his shirtsleeve over his hand and wiped down the handset and buttons as well as he could to get rid of his own fingerprints, thinking about how glad he was he didn't use the phone outside his own apartment. Walking back across the street he got in his car and sat a few minutes to think of his next move.

He turned the key to start the car and was about to pull out when a black SUV with tinted windows rolled down the street and slowed in front of the convenience store. Eddie couldn't see any faces through the tinting but could tell the driver and passenger were both looking the other way towards the pay phone he had used less than five minutes earlier. The SUV sped up and drove down the street, turned right and disappeared into downtown.

Putting the car in gear he took off the other direction, looping around the capitol building, through the north side of the city near the university then winding his way around the west side for an hour before going home.

When he eventually got home he parked his car around the corner from his apartment building, walked the opposite way around the block back to the gate and went in. Inside the apartment he pulled the shades and for the first time in six months took the mahogany box out from under his bed that held his Glock 23 pistol and put the weapon under his pillow, loaded with a full magazine and a round in the chamber.

For twelve years Eddie had chased terrorists from his office in D.C., most of them on the other side of the globe. In those years he had pulled his service pistol in the line of duty only once when tips led them to an American who thought he was working for Al Qaeda and had built a bomb out of a pipe, ball bearings, and gunpowder.

The man's contact in the terrorist network was actually an undercover FBI agent and they arrested him as he attempted to plant the bomb at the Lincoln Memorial.

Eddie got in bed, still in his jeans and shirt, and stared at the ceiling, listening to the sound of every car that drove by.

EDDIE STAYED IN his apartment all day, even skipping his morning run. That night, he finally went out again. He took no chances with the same pay phone downtown to try the two remaining numbers from the phone bill, and he drove northwest towards Lake Travis and found a decent looking grocery store on a main road with easy access back to the highway. He left his car running on the side of the parking lot and watched the street as he dialed the third number.

"Domino's Pizza, can I take your order?" came from the other end of the line and Eddie hung up and dialed the final number. The first ring had barely started when a women's voice answered, an eager tone to her voice.

"Hello?"

"Hi, my name's Eddie Holland. Do you know Peter Miller?"

"Yes! I am! I mean, I do. Who is this? Where's Peter?"

"I'm trying to figure out where he is but I don't want to talk on the phone. Can you meet me?" he paused and could hear her breathing on the other end, her eagerness replaced with concern.

"Who did you say you were?" she said.

"I've been hired to find Peter," Eddie said. "We need to meet. You choose where, anywhere you'd feel safe."

There was a long pause while the woman thought.

"Ok," she finally said. "The Alamo."

"The Alamo? Are you serious?" Eddie asked. "You want me to drive to San Antonio?"

There was more silence on the other end of the phone line.

"Fine, the Alamo. Can't get much more public than that. How about noon tomorrow? Wait at the flagpole. I'll find you."

"Ok. Noon," and she hung up.

"The Alamo," he said to himself, "Great."

AT 11:45 THE next day Eddie had made the 90-minute drive down to San Antonio and stood across the street from the Alamo, leaning on a drug store wall drinking a soda and flipping through the San Antonio guidebook, trying to look as touristy as possible. He'd considered buying an oversized foam cowboy hat but decided that was overkill.

Right at noon, a woman with red hair and wearing a yellow sundress walked up to the flagpole. She stood at the base and looked up to the top of it then started looking all around her, watching every man that walked towards her.

"Subtle," he thought, and crossed the street, pausing in the middle for a minivan with Oklahoma plates to go by while all the occupants stared out the right side windows at the Alamo. He moved up the other side of the plaza and then walked across the front of the building, looking down at the guidebook, then back up at the light brown stone walls, then back at the book until he was only a few feet from the woman.

She stood staring at him while he was looking up at the side of the old fort.

"Stop staring at me and walk across the street and stop at the corner," he said, still not looking at her.

"Why? I said the Alamo."

"Again, stop staring at me and go. I need to watch and make sure you weren't followed, but it doesn't do any good if you keep talking to me."

After a moment she looked back up the flagpole at the Texas flag flapping in the wind. Then she took off walking across the courtyard towards the street, looked both ways then walked across to the corner and stood there, trying not to look back at him.

Eddie had turned the direction she was walking, pretending to read the guidebook and watching people around her as she walked past them. He waited several minutes while she stood on the corner before being sure nobody was watching her.

Once across the courtyard he headed towards the opposite street corner. She was watching him now and he motioned with his head for her to walk down the sidewalk on the other side of the street. At the next signal, he crossed and walked up to her, standing face-to-face for the first time.

She was about five foot five and a 150 pounds. Her red hair was natural and the Texas sun was doing a job on her light skin. He considered for a moment buying her the oversized foam cowboy hat, but again decided against it.

"Who are you?" she asked.

"Eddie Holland. I've been hired to find Peter."

"Then you don't know where he is?" she said.

"No. That's why I'm trying to find him," Eddie said, the conversation was not being overly productive.

"When was the last time you saw him?" Eddie said.

"Three weeks ago. We'd gone out on Saturday night to a movie. He was supposed to call me Sunday afternoon to make plans, but I never heard from him"

"Let's go sit somewhere, this might take a while," he said and led her down the street towards the Riverwalk, a touristy area filled with chain restaurants and boat rides through an artificial canal. They took a table at a chain Tex-Mex restaurant and a bubbly waitress came by and sat down a big bowl of chips and salsa and asked if they'd like any drinks.

"Amaretto sour, please," the redhead said with no hesitation. Eddie grinned and ordered a Shiner Bock.

She told Eddie her name was Dorothy Jefferies but she went by Dot and she worked at BaseCamp Technologies. He explained what he knew so far, which wasn't much and that Peter Miller hadn't been heard from for a few weeks. He left out the part about the phone call and the black SUV and especially about hiding in his apartment with a loaded gun.

"So, fill in the blanks. What don't I know?" Eddie asked.

"Well, I worked with Pete at BaseCamp. We were in different departments but I knew who he was," she paused to take a sip from the cocktail that had been placed in front of her.

"Worked? As in past tense?" Eddie asked.

"Yeah. He got fired a few days before he disappeared."

"Did you tell anyone he was missing? Did you try calling the police?" Eddie said.

"No. I just figured he needed some time to himself. He seemed fine when we went to the movie, but I could tell losing his job shook him. He'd been there for a few years and really liked it."

"For three weeks he's been gone and you haven't called anyone?"

"I know. Now it seems like I could have done more, but I really didn't know what to do."

"Ok, so keep going," Eddie said.

"Peter and I started dating while he was at BaseCamp. I wasn't even sure he knew who I was for a long time. I'd see him at happy hours occasionally but never talked to him," she took another sip. "Then one day I waited by his car outside the office after work and I asked him out. Our first date was here, to the Alamo. I hadn't been down here since I was a kid."

"Do you have a photo of Peter?"

"You don't have one? How are you supposed to find him if you don't know what he looks like?" she asked while opening her purse to look.

"I haven't gotten the full file yet," Eddie lied.

"Here you go, that's him and me in Corpus Christi. We we're always going places," she said. "He loved going down to the beach. The south coast, he calls it."

Eddie looked at the picture taken on the beach. Dot wore a one-piece bathing suit with the skirt around her waist. Peter Miller stood just behind her to the side in bathing trunks. He was tall and had a runner's body but with more muscle, thick brown hair, and wore small, frameless sunglasses.

"What did you do in Corpus?" Eddie asked.

"We ate a lot, finding every café or restaurant with an ocean view. One morning we got up really early and went on a dolphin watching boat trip. It was magical," Dot's eyes were wide and her smile wider. "Whenever we went to the gulf I always insisted on doing a dolphin watching trip."

"Sounds like you did everything together."

"Well, almost. He's likes to jog and I, well, I'm not much of an athlete as you can probably tell," Dot said.

"So when you'd go places, he'd go jogging by himself?"

"Oh yeah, I didn't mind. I would usually just take my time getting ready or even go down to the beach or pool."

"How long would he jog?"

"Usually at least an hour," Dot said. "Though, between you and me, I don't know how much jogging he actually did. I went down to the beach one morning while he was out and I saw him come back in a cab and get dropped off down the street from our hotel. I guess he went further than he should have."

Eddie sat for a moment considering the new information.

"Did he ever talk about learning to fly?"

"No, not that I can think of."

His questions about Peter Miller were creating more questions than answers.

"Did you stay at his house a lot? You know, when you weren't driving all over Texas?" Eddie asked.

"I always went to his place. I invited him to my condo all the time but he said he preferred to be at his house," Dot deflated a bit admitting this. "And nobody at work knew we were dating. He wanted it that way. Said he hates the gossip mill and just thought it would be best."

"Tell me about when Peter got fired from BaseCamp," Eddie tried to move on to a new topic and away from relationship counseling.

"He worked in a wing of the building requiring top level security access, so any information coming out of there is always filtered," she said. "The rumor around the building is that he went ballistic on his boss, a VP, when they started questioning his work and he threw everything from the guy's desk and resisted the security guards when they came to escort him out. Then the police came and waited outside to make sure he didn't come back in."

"Does that seem in character for Peter?" Eddie asked.

"No, it really doesn't. Peter is a very calm person, very reserved."

"What do you do at BaseCamp?"

"I'm an assistant to one of the VP's. There are several. I don't even go to any staff meetings or have any real security access. I answer phones, make appointments—and that's about it."

The two talked for a while longer with not much coming from it, just more about their drives to the gulf and how Peter never went to Dot's condo. Eddie paid the check and they left the restaurant.

Eddie drove back to Austin with his mind churning over the new information, deciding he was further behind than he was before meeting Dot. He thought of all the things Peter Miller hid from his girlfriend.

He followed Dot's car up I-35 from several cars back and a different lane at all times. Keeping an eye on her car he watched all the other vehicles around her to see if anybody was following. As they hit Austin city limits and he'd seen nothing suspicious, he left the highway an exit before his and zigzagged through two neighborhoods before going home.

CHAPTER 7

Eddie got off the elevator in his sister's building and winked at the receptionist who rolled her eyes at him then watched him as he walked down the hallway and into Shelley's office that she shared with three other paralegals.

"I need you to call the phone company and get the address for a pay phone in Round Rock for me."

"Why don't you do it?" she asks.

"Because you can call and say the big long scary name of the law firm you work for and they might actually tell you."

"Good point. Give me the number," she replied while looking up the telephone company's number online and dialed it. After a few minutes of being transferred and another few minutes on hold after telling the person on the other end of the line who she worked for, she scribbled an address onto a notepad on her desk.

"You're the best," Eddie said, grabbing the paper as he jumped up and kissed Shelley on the top of her head and practically ran out the door.

The drive up to Round Rock was uneventful and Eddie exited into town and started watching street names. After a few turns and a bit of help from some kids hanging out on a corner, he found the street and then moved slowly down it looking for the building. He stopped when he reached a row of shops and a liquor store then he saw the building number on a place called Palace Bar at the far end. He parked across the street and settled into his seat to watch the door from his rearview mirror for a while.

After almost an hour of watching the bar nobody had entered or left. He got out of his car and headed across the street and opened the dark, solid door and walked through. Eddie moved towards the bar and sat on a stool. After a few seconds a Chinese man came out of the back room and walked behind the bar and stopped and stared at Eddie.

"Corona," Eddie said. The bartender looked over Eddie's shoulder then nodded slightly and turned and took a bottle of beer from the fridge behind the bar. He popped the cap and pushed a lime wedge into the open top and sat it in front of Eddie.

Sipping the beer, he began to take in the rest of the room. The neon signs were in Chinese, and a few worn-out posters on the walls were as well. Looking around some more, he saw two men in a booth in the dark, far corner of the room that he hadn't seen before. They wore silk shirts, one white and the other red. The men were looking back at Eddie and he kept looking around the room like he hadn't noticed them.

He finished his beer and asked where the bathroom was and got up to walk the direction the bartender had pointed. He walked past the two men in the booth and into a long, narrow hallway that held several doors and at the far end a beat up pay phone. He picked up the receiver while holding the hook down with his finger then lifted the hook and listened as the dial tone sounded through the earpiece. He hung up the phone. Finding the door marked men, he went in and spent enough time that it was conceivable he'd gone to the bathroom, then washed his hands and walked back out to the bar. He put a 10-dollar bill down on the bar, and walked out the front door.

Not knowing the town, he felt uncomfortable about winding through the streets to watch behind him, but did his best while backtracking to the highway. Forty-five minutes later he was back in Austin and sitting at a different bar drinking a far better beer and thinking about the one he'd been in earlier. Knowing the bartender here, he asked and used the cordless telephone and called Gus then finished his first beer then nursed his second while he waited.

Gus walked in and the two took their own booth in a somewhat quiet corner. Eddie told him about the pay phone number from the phone bill, the black SUV, and the Chinese bar in Round Rock. He did not tell him about the pistol he had in a holster clipped to the back of his belt underneath his T-shirt. Even though they were best friends Gus was an active federal agent and it's still illegal to carry a concealed firearm in a bar in Texas. Though if Eddie had to guess, Gus had his Sig Sauer P229 under his jacket, since there was no other reason to be wearing a jacket.

Gus leaned back in his seat, looked up at the fake Tiffany light that hung low over their table and shook his head.

"What have you gotten into?" Gus asked.

"I don't know. That's why I'm talking to you. Do you know something? Have you heard of Palace Bar?"

"I haven't heard of that bar specifically, but we've been alerted in the last few years about Chinese gang activity moving into the area. Round Rock is a bit of a stretch, and not really where I'd expect to hear they were setting up shop, but it is also way too much of a coincidence."

"Shit," Eddie said, looking at his empty beer bottle. "Chinese gangs, huh."

"Yeah," Gus said. "Chinese gangs. But it gets weirder."

"How is that possible?"

"Our office got a call from D.C. today urging the Austin field office to take a lot of interest in a local missing person's case."

"Peter Miller?" Eddie asked.

"Nope. A man named Gerry Howard."

"Who the hell is Gerry Howard?"

"He's the CEO of BaseCamp Technology," Gus said. "And my SAC put me on it."

"So what are the odds of two different men from the same company in Austin going missing and it not being connected?" Eddie asked, knowing the answer. "Who made the call from D.C. asking for the field office to look into it?"

"A U.S. Senator. He's an old college friend of Gerry Howard's," Gus said.

"What are you doing Sunday morning?"

"I would usually sleep late but sounds like those plans are changing," Gus knew Eddie's problems were about to become his.

CHAPTER 8

Eddie woke up Saturday morning to the sound of the alarm on his nightstand. He dressed and grabbed a gym bag from the floor of his closet and left his apartment and drove north from Austin where the strip malls are replaced by farmland dotted with horses and cattle. The road names become numbers and the only other vehicles were tractors and pickups. The old VW felt solid and the motor purred with ease along the small state roads.

An hour later the strip malls appeared again, as did the fast food restaurants and low slung brick houses as he entered Killeen, Texas, and continued through the town until he pulled up to a gate guarded by men who looked like boys in green army uniforms with black rifles. One of the soldiers approached the small car.

"Eddie Holland to see Major Clem Akins," Eddie said. He handed his driver's license to the guard.

A phone call was made inside the guard booth and the south gate to Fort Hood slid open and Eddie drove through. He wound his way around the U.S. Army post until he reached a grey building with no markings on the west edge, got out of the car, and grabbed his gym bag from the passenger seat then walked through the sliding metal door into the building.

"I wasn't sure you'd make it," a voice boomed from the darkness inside the building.

"I wasn't either, honestly," Eddie said. "But I need this."

"Need," the man emerged from the darkness into the stream of light coming from the door. "I don't think I've ever heard anyone say they 'need' this."

"Good to see you, Clem," Eddie said. The men shook hands, Clem's left hand going to Eddie's right shoulder and holding there for a moment.

"Good to see you, too," Clem said.

"Okay, well let's get this thing going," Eddie said.

The Army captain smiled and pointed towards the room to their right; Eddie went in to change, returning a few minutes later in tan fatigue pants, boots, and a skintight tan tee shirt with the faded logo of the Army Rangers on the front.

Clem turned and saw Eddie's shirt and laughed.

"You still have that old thing?" Clem said.

"I won it fair and square," Eddie said.

"You gonna give me a chance to win it back today?"

"Aren't you getting a little old to play with the boys?" Eddie said.

"If it weren't for this, I'd gladly go a few rounds with you," Clem said. He made a fist and tapped his right thigh. Through the thick fatigue pants you could hear the hollow sound of the titanium limb that replaced his real leg several years earlier.

"Even with that I'm not confident I could take you," Eddie said. "You haven't slowed a bit."

Clem hit a row of breaker switches in a rusty box on the wall, and the lights came on one at a time, revealing the contents of the building. In the far corner was an obstacle course of rope walls, tires, a zip line, and an area of razor wire elevated a foot or so off of the ground. Right in front of them was a 20 square foot wrestling mat that had been salvaged from a small town high school that was being torn down. To the far right was a series of targets for live-fire shooting exercises.

"I'm surprised they let you keep this place," Eddie said.

"It stays off their radar mostly," Clem said. "I don't take any money from the budget for it. Plus the base commander always acts like he owes me something."

Eddie stretched his shoulders and back against a steel pole.

"So, where do you want to start?" Clem said.

"It's your house," Eddie said.

Clem led Eddie to the obstacle course and after a few pointers set him on his way to tackle the ropes, tires, and razor wire, timing him on each pass. After a dozen times through the course, Eddie stopped and went back to Clem, who handed him a bottle of water.

"You're faster through there than half of my men, and they're 21 and 22 years old," Clem said. "You have fifteen years on them."

"Am I going to get to meet any of them today?" Eddie said.

"I selected a few who are especially used to abuse," Clem said. "Both giving and getting it."

"Excellent. I'm looking forward to it," Eddie said.

"Let's get some shooting in before they get here, though," Clem said.

Moving to the other end of the facility the captain unlocked and opened a cabinet.

"Take your pick."

Eddie took an AR-15 rifle off the wall and sighted it from his right shoulder.

"That's a nice weapon, but I don't run into those in the field as much as you guys," Eddie said. He put the rifle back on the wall and picked up the Beretta M9 pistol.

"This is more like it," Eddie said. "This isn't a 90's model is it?"

"Sure isn't, I've gotten rid of any of the older ones with a history of malfunctioning," Clem said.

Eddie popped the magazine out and loaded it with fifteen rounds from a box in the cabinet, slammed the magazine back into the grip of the standard issue Army pistol then pulled the slide back firmly and released it, bringing the first round up into the chamber for firing. He took the leather holster and belt off the hook in the cabinet and strapped it around his waist.

"Shall we shoot something?" Eddie said.

"I thought you'd never ask," Clem said. He pulled his own M9 out of its holster on his hip, checked that the magazine was full, and loaded the chamber.

The men worked through the live-fire range as they had for years, the wooden targets mimicking terrorists, bank robbers, kidnappers or whatever they had in their minds as they methodically took the bad guys out. They covered one another as they hid behind barriers and moved forward, the cracks of the nine-millimeter guns being fired echoed inside the old metal building.

They reached the final obstacle that was new to Eddie, a cinder block wall with a single wooden door. Eddie didn't know what was on the other side but was sure his old friend and fighting partner had arranged something to throw him off.

Eddie looked at Clem who took up a defensive position and signaled him to breach the doorway.

With a single solid kick just below the handle the door flew open and Eddie ran in and moved to his right, gun raised and scanning the room. The door swung shut behind him from a spring-loaded hinge the captain had installed the night before and the room was in complete darkness.

Eddie held still and slowed his breathing. Even though it was a controlled target range situation his pulse was elevated and every piece of stimuli was diverting his attention. Keeping his sounds as muffled as possible he started to move to his right in the darkness, his forefinger stretched onto the trigger guard to avoid a misfire.

A single sound came from in front of him, the scuff of a boot on the floor, but enough for Eddie. This wasn't a target simulation. There were real live soldiers in the darkness and Eddie quietly placed the pistol into its holster on his hip.

Another boot scuff on the floor ahead of him and Eddie gauged the distance in the darkness, took a step then fell into a forward roll, letting his back run at a slight angle across the floor rather than down his spine. As his feet came over he brought his left leg under him, braced his left hand on the floor and extended his right leg into a kick with full power and felt his boot hit solid. The man on the receiving end grunted as the wind was knocked partly out of him. Eddie felt the man's arm come under his foot to try to flip him into a vulnerable position.

While his foot was being lifted he used the momentary support and rotated his body and brought his left leg around at ground level, sweeping the assailants leg. The sound of the man's body hitting the concrete floor was painful, but this is what they train for. Eddie dropped to the man and put his forearm across the opponent's throat to simulate choking him out and the soldier followed drill protocols and stayed still on the floor, now a casualty in the war game.

The man he had taken down was the point and somewhere not far behind him would be two more soldiers spreading through the room, if Clem hadn't misdirected him by saying he had a few soldiers for Eddie to meet. His opponents had heard the struggle and had a better idea of where Eddie was than he did of their locations.

Still kneeling beside the soldier he'd taken out, Eddie untied his boots and slipped them off then took them with him as he stood and stepped forward in silence in his socks. He took one of the boots by the end of the long laces and began swinging the heavy boot to his side then flicked his wrist and released it. The boot flew through the darkness and hit the floor. Two sets of feet turned on the concrete and Eddie could tell he wasn't far from one of them.

Suspecting they had turned away from him towards the sound of the boot, Eddie took three fast steps forward until he could smell the man right in front of him, the back of his head inches from Eddie's face. He tossed the other boot around in front of the man and it hit the floor right at his feet. The soldier jumped and took a step back into Eddie. Eddie brought his left hand up around the front of the man landing his palm onto his opponent's chin and whispered in his ear.

"You're dead."

The man relaxed his body to fall to the floor but Eddie held him up and with his free right hand snapped his fingers once.

The last remaining soldier turned to the sound and moved towards it. He stepped in with a kick that landed in his teammate's stomach. Eddie stepped right, letting the body fall, and threw three punches into the dark air. The first two landed in the chest of his final opponent, the third was caught and his arm was turned against the elbow joint and doubled Eddie over. A pair of kicks landed in his gut but before the expected elbow came down into the back of his head Eddie rolled forward out of the hold and extended his legs up and trapped the man's head between his calves and let the momentum carry the soldier to the floor. Eddie spun his body and bent his knees back behind him as he pulled the pistol from its holster and brought barrel of the Beretta nine millimeter to the top the man's head.

"Bang," Eddie said.

The lights came on as the door swung open and the captain stepped in. Eddie got his first look around and saw the three soldiers getting to their feet.

"Impressive," Clem said. "But one of them kicked you a couple times. You're slipping."

"Great exercise," Eddie said. "I had no idea what you were sending me in to."

"You ready to hit the mat and do some real one-on-one with these boys?"

"Let's do it," Eddie said.

CHAPTER 9

Eddie and Gus sat down from Palace Bar in an unmarked cruiser from the FBI's auto pool.

"So, why are we on a stake out in a cop car?" Eddie asked.

"If we were in one of our cars and got spotted, they'd have our make and model and our tags. These gangs are connected and can get addresses faster than I can on the computer at my desk back at HQ. If we get spotted in this, they just see another black Crown Vic with no hubcaps and think local PD is watching them again."

"Well, I like the part about not finding out my address," Eddie said.

"Thanks for your approval, it means so much to me," Gus said. "You think maybe Peter Miller and Gerry Howard had some bad bets with a gang and they…" Gus made the shape of a gun with his forefinger and thumb and pointed it at his own forehead.

"I don't know, it isn't like I hung out with Peter, but from what I learned about him he doesn't seem like he'd place bets with a bookie at a gang bar."

Eddie stopped talking as a black SUV pulled up in front of Palace Bar. The large truck blocked their view of the bar door. The man in the front passenger seat got out and looked both ways on the sidewalk and street. He was Chinese and large in the chest with shoulders like a bodybuilder. He opened the back passenger side door on the far side of the vehicle keeping Eddie and Gus from seeing anything.

"Is that the SUV you saw in Austin?" Gus asked.

"I don't know, it's Texas, a black SUV is standard issue for every soccer mom, but it sure could be."

The man from the front passenger seat stepped to the front of the car and stood watching the road. Even though the unmarked squad car was several doors down on the opposite side of the road it was unlikely the man did not see it. He was there doing a job, and both Eddie and Gus recognized that job as bodyguard.

The door to the bar opened and a slim Chinese man in a black suit walked out and disappeared behind the open SUV door.

As the bodyguard turned back towards the door to the truck, his suit jacket lifted in the breeze and the stock of a black pistol was visible for a moment before being covered again. Once the passenger was safe in the back seat the bodyguard stepped to the front of the SUV and looked straight across at Eddie and Gus, holding the gaze for several moments, then turned and climbed in the front seat and the driver pulled out and disappeared down the street.

"Did you get the license plate?" Eddie asked.

"Yeah," Gus said. "I'll run it in the morning."

CHAPTER 10

Jimmy Finch was born in Plano, Texas, and moved to South Padre Island after high school and a few semesters of business classes at the community college with dreams of owning his own bar on the beach. He'd been down to the island a few times with friends to drink heavily on spring breaks and summer road trips.

He didn't own a bar yet but had worked up to manager at one owned by a local whose day-to-day interest in the establishment had diminished. The decor was typical beach town kitsch with a kayak hanging on one wall, a fishing net taking up most of the ceiling and music supplied by the entire catalogue of Jimmy Buffett.

What the place had that no other did on the island was a non-existent back wall that opened onto the gulf. The rear patio, really an extension of the bar floor, continued right out and angled down to where it touched the low surf of the water. Deck chairs were regularly dragged several feet into the water where bar patrons would sit and have margaritas and beers brought right out to them.

At the end of a busy night, the party gang had moved on to other parties and Jimmy was sweeping up, having let everyone else go home. He felt it showed initiative and won support of the staff so hopefully one day he would be the manager. With nobody there to see, he kept sweeping right out the back and pushed the dust, crumbs and all the other dirt the wide shop broom had gathered right into the water. On the third stroke of shoving the detritus away his broom hit something. And on the next stroke it snagged.

Jimmy pulled the broom but it didn't respond. He pulled a small flashlight out of his pocket, always on hand due to the frequent power outages the island experienced, he shined the light on the water as he squatted down to pull the broom head free. Reaching into the dark liquid his hand fell on something solid. He grabbed and pulled, falling backwards as the object gave way. Lying on his back he looked at the item resting on his stomach and he screamed as the flashlight shined on the severed human arm.

CHAPTER 11

Eddie was in bed but not sleeping at five o'clock in the morning when there was a quiet knock on his apartment door. His hand slipped easily under the unused pillow on the other side of the bed and gripped the stock of his pistol. Laying still he waited until the knock was repeated and he stepped out of bed and moved through the darkness towards his front door, staying close to the wall and away from the line-of-site of the peephole. Once he was leaning on the doorjamb on the hinged side of the door he paused and slowed his breathing to be able to listen better.

Just as he had calmed the knock came again causing him to jump then he heard the voice whispering loudly, "Eddie… open the door."

He relaxed and stared at the ceiling for a moment then stepped over and opened the door to reveal Gus standing on the opposite side of the wall from where Eddie had been, his right hand behind his back, most likely resting on the grip of his own service pistol while he watched the apartment complex courtyard below and other doors for movement. Once he saw Eddie had opened the door he walked through the opening and pulled the door from Eddie's grip, closing it quickly and quietly.

"There's been a development," Gus said. "More than one, actually."

"Oh?" Eddie said.

"First, I ran the license plate from the SUV at the bar," Gus said. "It's registered to a company in Houston. When I checked the address of the business it came up as a mailbox at an independent package shipping store."

"Strange, but not unheard of," Eddie said.

"True, but there's no other records for the company," Gus said. "No licenses, no physical addresses, nothing with the IRS and no social security records."

"Could it be a foreign business and just have no real U.S. presence?" Eddie said.

"It could but if they are doing any business here then there would be some kind of trail," Gus said.

"What else do you have?" Eddie said.

"I was at the office working late when I heard a few agents getting loud, talking about something that had just come across the wire," Gus said.

Gus drew a curtain back slightly, checking out the courtyard once again while talking.

"Why are you so jumpy?" Eddie said.

"Because you've gotten me mixed up with, well, whatever this is," Gus said. "About three hours ago South Padre PD was called to a bar on the beach. The closing manager found a body washed up from the gulf behind the place."

"Is it Peter Miller or Gerry Howard?" Eddie asked.

"No positive ID yet but with two missing men on our hands, seems like more than a coincidence."

"Peter Miller also has a connection to Padre. He and his girlfriend go down for long weekends," Eddie said. "We have a cause of death?"

"Preliminary from the scene is gunshot to the abdomen but the ME's office hasn't said anything yet."

"That's a slow death," Eddie said. "He most likely drowned before bleeding out."

Gus nodded, "Get dressed. We're going to the beach."

THE TEXAS STATE Police Gulfstream airplane took off from Austin at 9:00 a.m. and headed towards Brownsville, the closest city with an airstrip that could handle that size aircraft. From there, they transferred to a border patrol helicopter for the fifteen-minute hop over to South Padre Island.

Once in the helicopter with only the ICE pilots Eddie turned to Gus and talked through the microphone on his oversized earphones.

"How'd you talk the bureau into letting you follow this?"

"Remember I told you about the call from D.C. about Gerry Howard?" Gus said. "That call was from a senate office, a high ranking member of the intelligence committee. Any possible leads on this missing man, we follow."

They landed by a one story building in Port Isabel, Texas, just across the bridge from South Padre Island. The two got out of the helicopter and waved at the pilot who had the skids off the ground and headed west before Gus and Eddie even got to the door to the county medical examiner's office.

Eddie flinched at the smell as he and Gus walked into the coroner's lab. Gus had no visible reaction. The body was all on one table but in two parts. The arm that Jimmy Finch had found was the bodies right arm and lay where it should have been in relation to the rest of the body except with a six-inch gap in between them. The face was half gone, partly from fish feeding on the corpse and partly from whatever took the arm off.

The coroner walked through the door on the other side of the lab and up to the table, standing across from Eddie and Gus.

"They were very lucky to recover the rest of the body. Generally when you find a limb it's nowhere near the heavier torso, but it appears the separation probably occurred closer to the recovery spot, perhaps held together by the shirt sleeve."

"How did it get separated, is it a shark bite?" Eddie asked.

"No, nothing so glamorous," the coroner responded. "See the marks on the arm here, and on the shoulder? If it had been a shark, those would not be as clean. Sharks grab on and dive and saw through bone. These marks are too even. This was most likely done by the propeller of a large boat." The coroner had picked up the loose arm and showed them the end, much more closely than Eddie would have preferred.

"What about the gunshot? Was a bullet recovered?" Gus asked.

The coroner moved over to the torso and with a shiny silver tool probed the entry point of the bullet on the man's abdomen, just below his chest.

"It obviously entered here but there's an exit wound on his lower back, just below his tailbone, so no projectile was recovered. From the size of the holes I'm guessing it was a nine millimeter."

"Any progress on getting an ID?" Gus asked.

"State Police took the fingerprints as soon as the body arrived here but I haven't heard anything yet."

Eddie looked at the body, taking in the shape and size and thinking about the photo of Peter and Dot.

"I can tell you who it isn't," he said. "It isn't Peter Miller."

Eddie and Gus left the coroner's office and a patrol car gave them a ride across the bridge into Padre and dropped them off at a motel a few blocks from the water.

"Tell them we sent you, they'll give you a good rate," the officer said.

"Sure thing, and thanks for the ride," Gus said to him as the white police cruiser with blue and yellow stripes down the side sped off faster than it needed to.

The pair made their way to the motel office and rented two rooms. Gus went upstairs to his room and Eddie walked down the sidewalk to his on the street level, went in, and dropped his bag on the bed. He sat in the wooden chair beside the window-mounted air conditioner for less than a minute then got up and locked the door behind him. He ran up the steps to the second level and knocked on Gus's door.

"Feel like a beer?" Eddie said when Gus opened the door.

"You read my mind," Gus locked his door and the two men went back to the motel office and asked the clerk to get them a cab. An older Ford Explorer with taxi markings pulled up a short time later and Eddie described where he wanted to go to the driver. Four minutes later the annoyed cabbie collected his six dollar fare and let the two men out in front of the Gulf View Bar and Grill.

"Why here?" Gus asked.

"This is where the body was found. You have a picture of Gerry Howard?"

"Of course I do," They walked into the bar, which was over crowded even for middle of the afternoon.

"I guess having a dead body found at your bar makes you more popular around these parts," Eddie said.

"It's not like they found a dead rat, I guess," Gus said.

They worked their way to the bar and edged themselves through several shirtless college aged boys in swim trunks and took the two remaining bar stools. Eddie motioned to the young bartender who eventually worked himself over to them, but not too quickly, knowing the inebriated shirtless fraternity brothers were likely to be better tippers than the two older guys who looked like cops.

"What'll it be, guys?" The bartender asked.

"Corona for me," Gus said.

"I'll taken a margarita on the rocks with salt, top shelf," Eddie said.

Gus looked at Eddie after he'd ordered the margarita.

"What! I'm feeling the beach vibe down here. They got Jimmy Buffet playing and look at that view," Eddie said, pointing to the back of the room.

"Wow. That is impressive," Gus said and they stared at the nonexistent back wall and the wide-open view of the Gulf of Mexico. Then they stared at the dozen or so college girls in bikinis all holding beer bottles at head height all dancing to the music with the gulf water up to their knees.

"One corona and one margarita, guys," The bartender sat the drinks on the bar. "That'll be $13."

"Keep the change, if we can ask you a few questions," Eddie handed two twenty-dollar bills to the bartender. "You Jimmy Finch?"

"Yeah, I am," Jimmy said. "What kind of questions? If it was about last night, I told the cops everything I knew, which isn't much."

"You ever see either of these guys before?" Eddie said, handing him his copy of Peter Miller's photo while Gus handed him Gerry Howard's.

Jimmy Finch spent a while looking at each photograph and started shaking his head.

"Nah, neither of these guys looks familiar, the girl either," Jimmy said, referencing the photo of Peter Miller with Dot. "We get a lot of faces through here, but I'm pretty good at remembering them."

CHAPTER 12

Eddie woke early in his motel room in South Padre. He grabbed shorts, socks and his running shoes from the backpack he'd thrown together before they flew out the day before and took the opportunity for a run on the beach. The sun was barely up and he ran easily in the sand, his lungs filling and emptying of the gulf's salty air, the occasional smell of fish on the morning breeze.

After several miles Eddie slowed to a stop and rested his hands on his knees, hanging his head down. He didn't need to catch his breath but felt he should at least look like the run had taken something out of him so he didn't make the other morning joggers feel badly. Looking back up at the open water, an early morning dolphin watching cruise boat created a small white wake.

Replaying the night before through his mind he was debating if the man's body was Gerry Howard when he heard the elated sounds of people on the boat far off the shore as a trio of dolphins breached a few feet off of the stern. His thoughts went to Dot, then to Peter, then to Mexico.

SHOWERED AND DRESSED in the same jeans he'd worn the day before, a fresh 'Keep Austin Weird' T-shirt from his backpack and his brown pork-pie hat, he found Gus at the motel coffee shop with a view of the pool. Gus took a long drink of his coffee with a splash of milk.

"Local chief called me while you were running," Gus said. "They got an ID on the body."

"Tell me it isn't Gerry Howard," Eddie said.

"It's Gerry Howard."

"Well, hell. This sure isn't the direction I wanted this case to take," Eddie said.

"I have to stay down here another day or two to follow up and see if I can learn anything. I checked with my contact at State Police for you and no luck on a fast ride back to Austin with them, so you can either rent a car or hop on a commercial prop-jet out of Brownsville," Gus said.

Eddie chewed on a big bite of pancakes covered with fake maple syrup and swallowed. He chased it with a swig of coffee.

"I think I'll hang out down here for a few days," Eddie said.

"You think Peter Miller might be here?" Gus was interrupted by his cell phone vibrating on the table and answered.

"Yeah, he's with me. Hold on," Gus said into the phone after listening for a few seconds then handed his phone to Eddie with a disgusted look. "Seriously, you have to get a phone."

"Hello?" Eddie said into the phone.

"Where the hell are you?" His sister's voice came screaming through the earpiece. "I've been all over looking for you."

"I'm in South Padre," Eddie replied.

"Great fucking time for a vacation but somehow you actually went the right direction for once," she said.

"What do you mean?" Eddie asked.

"Some chick named Dot called my cell looking for you," Shelley said.

He listened to his sister for the next two minutes without interrupting, motioning to Gus for his pad and pen he kept with him at all times and wrote down a few words.

"You're the best, thank you."

Eddie hit the end button on Gus's Blackberry and handed it back to him. "I'm going to Mexico."

"Is it about Peter Miller?"

"It's not just about Peter Miller, it is Peter Miller."

Gus sat silently staring at Eddie with a blank expression for the better part of a minute.

"Then I'm going with you," Gus said.

CHAPTER 13

Peter Miller sat in the back corner of a bar in Matamoros, Mexico, just off of the main shopping street where American tourists visit to get their Mexican adventure without having to go more than 10 miles into the country. There was just enough fair-complexioned people that he didn't stand out and he drank just enough to keep the bartender from caring he was there far too long.

It was more than three weeks ago that Peter had left his home in Austin without calling his girlfriend to tell her where he was heading, and it was six days since he had killed Gerry Howard on a remote beach on South Padre Island.

Peter sipped a Corona Light even though he'd have preferred tequila but didn't want to get drunk. He just needed to keep his nerves calm from the shock of having shot a man and to prepare for finally telling somebody about it. He was thinking about the phone call he made the night before to Dot, her excitement at hearing from him and then her fears of what was happening to him. She told Peter about Eddie Holland and their meeting at the Alamo and that she thinks he can trust Eddie. She then spoke for several minutes and Peter didn't hear her while he was thinking about what to do, who to trust, and how to come out the other side safely.

He didn't tell her about Gerry Howard and the beach. He did tell her to call Eddie Holland.

CHAPTER 14

Eddie and Gus drove across the bridge from Brownsville into Mexico in a rented Toyota Highlander. Each of them had a backpack full of dirty clothes and a few hundred dollars they pulled from an ATM in South Padre. Eddie had his Glock 23 and Gus had his Sig Sauer P229 Tactical pistol. Both guns were hidden up under the dash of the SUV to get across the border, which they did with no problem.

Eddie parked near the tourist area in a space facing the exit of the parking lot. They retrieved their pistols and clipped their holsters in their belts in their lower backs and let their shirts hang over the weapons.

Gus glanced at the GPS map on his Blackberry and quickly described the street layout to Eddie and they walked off in separate directions.

As planned, Gus arrived at the bar first, blending in with the locals and the tourists with ease. It was a wide room with no wall in the front, just a pair of garage doors that pulled down when the place closed late each night. He sat at a small table near the front, and with a motion of his hand and a nod to the bartender, a tall glass of beer was brought over to him.

Gus surveyed the room, taking in the beer posters and neon signs and outdated advertisements for Latino bands that played in the larger cities away from the border towns. Without stopping his moving gaze of the walls he saw a white man sitting in the back with a couple of empty Corona bottles on his table who was staring intently at the wide open façade of the bar. The man checked his watch twice within a minute and Gus knew it was Peter Miller.

He let his attention move away and continue across the room, looking to see if anyone was watching Peter or had noticed him watching Peter. After several minutes and no obvious signs of a third party, Gus leaned back in his chair facing the opening of the bar to the street.

Eddie stood across the street leaning on the front of a clothing store that specialized in school uniforms for the local children. The front door of the store was open and the frosty air conditioning spilled out onto him relieving him momentarily from the 110-degree heat. He had a line of sight to Gus sitting 60 feet away, through the gaps in two street carts selling various Mexican foods. A few moments later, Gus picked up his cell phone and checked the display, then set it back on his table, signaling Eddie that Peter Miller was there.

Eddie worked his way through the food carts and waited as an old Ford pickup passed on the street, walked into the bar, winding through the randomly placed tables without making eye contact with Gus and sat down facing Peter Miller.

"I'm Eddie Holland," he said.

Peter Miller sat straight up staring at him, taken off guard by his directness.

"Why don't you tell me how we got to this point, sitting in a bar in Mexico," Eddie said. "And did you play role in the death of Gerry Howard?"

Peter looked down at his hands and the blood drained from his face.

"I'll take that as a yes."

"So they found him?" Peter Miller said.

"Yeah, they found him. Twice actually. Or more accurately the two parts of him," Eddie said.

"What! I didn't… I mean I shot him but I didn't…"

"I know. Looks like while floating in the gulf, a boat motor took his arm off," Eddie said.

"I think I'm going to be sick," Peter said, turning the beer bottle around in his hand.

Eddie turned in his chair and nodded to Gus who stood and walked to their table with his half empty beer bottle and sat down.

"Who's this? Who are you?" Peter got flustered at the new, unexpected face. "Dot didn't say there would be anyone else."

"This is Gus. He's my oldest friend, he's a man you can trust, and he's a Special Agent with the FBI," Eddie said.

"I need to hear your story, Peter, if you were connected to the death of Gerry Howard in South Padre," Gus explained. "We're in Mexico, I have no jurisdiction to arrest you. I'm here to help Eddie and to help you if you need it."

Peter sat silent for a minute thinking and looking back and forth at the two men sitting across from him.

"Where should I start?" Peter said.

"As far back as you need," Gus said.

Peter drank from his beer bottle and stared out the open doors of the bar at the street for a moment then began.

"I'd been at BaseCamp several years and things were good," Peter said. "The people are great, the work is fun and it's everything I wanted to do. About six months ago I started noticing some irregular levels of network traffic, large amounts of data moving out of BaseCamp, generally late at night."

"And this was part of your job, noticing things like this?" Eddie said.

"Yeah, definitely. I was in charge of network security. We run a bulletproof network, have to with the level of classified data we deal with. When you start seeing something like this, a red flag pops up real quick," Peter took another drink of his beer.

"I went to see my boss, Gerry Howard, the next morning and told him what I'd found. He was concerned but more about the fact that I'd seen it happen. Then he told me that he was the one doing the transfers, that he was working closely with the NSA to provide more detailed information to them."

"What kind of information?" Gus said.

"BaseCamp builds the systems that the military uses to track satellites and collects all of the information being sent back and forth from all the different bases, airplanes, ships and even the Pentagon. You can track an individual Humvee from around the world, even a single soldier."

Gus had his notebook out and was quickly writing with his ballpoint pen.

"That's some pretty valuable data, something our enemies would love to have," Eddie said.

"Indeed," Peter said. "That's why we're so locked in with our contracts. The government doesn't want to switch to another company since we already have all this data. It's one of the few contracts that never has to go for renewal; it's automatically approved every year."

"Sounds like a great deal for BaseCamp," Gus said.

"Gerry told me he was impressed I had found the abnormality in network traffic. He'd set up the transfers himself and thought he'd done a good job masking it. So he asked me to help, that it had to be done in complete secrecy or the NSA would be very upset."

"And you agreed to help?" Eddie said.

"Of course I did," Peter said. "It was a great opportunity to impress my boss and even the NSA. It could mean a promotion, raise, or even moving on to a job in DC."

"So what did you have to do?" Gus said.

"I had to create a secure way to transfer all of our military data in a way that no other person at BaseCamp would notice it was happening. Being head of network security I knew who had access to dig in and find what I had found and I knew all of their skill levels and abilities. It was a breeze. I had a secure, invisible connection set up within three days.

"So a month goes by and I've processed four of these transfers, each Saturday night, late. I'd trigger it from home. I'm bored one night while doing it, and decide to see where exactly the transfer is going. I write a quick app and send it on its way, to trace the packet. It bounced around a lot, coast to coast, Europe, even hitting a server in South Africa at one point. It was impressive, looked like these NSA guys really knew their job. Then it landed."

"Landed?" Gus said.

"It ended, found where the transfer was going," Peter said.

"And where was it?" Eddie said.

"Beijing, China."

Eddie and Gus leaned back in their chairs and looked at each other then back at Peter Miller.

"What did you do?" Gus said.

"I called Gerry the next day, on Sunday. He met me downtown. I told him what I'd found. He was pissed at first, and then he calmed down. I could tell he was trying to do damage control. I assured him I had told nobody else. He said he was working on a big deal for BaseCamp, everything was above board, but he still needed complete discretion."

"Did you believe him?" Eddie said.

"By this time, not at all, but he was my boss, and the CEO of the company. What else could I do? Then he offered me a bonus each time I processed a transfer— except that I'd have to take a larger part in the process. Each week I'd receive a phone call on Sunday morning to confirm the data had been received. For that he'd give me 10 grand."

"A week? Ten grand a week for answering your phone?" Gus said.

"I knew he was just trying to buy me off, but ten grand a week is a lot. I still have student loans and would love to buy a house someday, so I said sure."

"What were you doing with the money?" Eddie said.

"I knew I couldn't just start buying stuff or pay my debts off that quickly, that would be too fishy. So I started putting it in safe deposit boxes until I could figure it out."

"Let me guess, you used banks in South Padre and Corpus Christi?" Eddie said.

"Yeah, how'd you know?"

"As I said, a guess."

"Then I got cold feet. I had well over $120,000 in cash sitting in multiple safe deposit boxes, I figured I didn't need any more money and just wanted to be clear of the situation. I made backups of all of the transfers and put them at an offsite data storage center where they would be secure, I logged everything I did, every conversation with Gerry and every penny he paid me in documents and stored them with the files. Then I went in to work to get myself fired. I figured if I didn't have access to the network, he couldn't get me to do the transfers anymore."

"How did you get yourself fired?" Eddie said.

"I had a regular weekly status meeting with a couple of the VP's. I went into the meeting with alcohol on my breath and acted belligerent towards them. Then I started yelling at them. Then I started throwing stuff off the desk of the VP's office we were in. I said a lot of really rude things about the picture of his wife right before I shattered it on the floor. Security finally came and escorted me out and the police were outside to make sure I didn't try to go back in."

"You may have missed your true calling as an actor," Eddie said. "But before we high-five you and all, there's still a dead body and we haven't heard about that yet."

"As soon as I got home Gerry showed up at my door. I told him I knew about China. He got pissed, told me I was messing everything up, that we would both go to prison or worse if I didn't find a way to keep sending the transfers. I told him I still had access, that I needed the money and would keep doing it, but needed more a week since I wasn't working at BaseCamp anymore and would have to hack into their network. He agreed, told me I'd better not be late by even a second on the next transfer and left.

"I decided to get out of town, grabbed the money I had hidden at my house and I drove to Padre and paid cash for a motel. I started getting nervous sitting in one place so I went to the banks where I had money in safe deposit boxes and took it all out and closed my accounts. But that was my mistake. It made me traceable. I was planning on leaving for Mexico the next morning."

"When was this?" Eddie said.

"About a week ago," Peter said.

CHAPTER 15

SIX DAYS EARLIER

Peter Miller sat in the back one of the many dive bars on South Padre Island, Texas. Not one of the beachfront hangouts for college kids on weekend trips and spring break, but one further off the gulf that catered to the people who lived on the island, worked on the island or came to the island to steal or take advantage of the college kids. This one was across the street from the motel he had paid $79 in cash for a room for the night before he fled into Mexico the next morning.

Six beers and three shots had been delivered to him over the last few hours and added to his tab, secured by a credit card being held behind the bar by a man in a tank top serving the watered down liquor. He had no intention of charging the tab to the card.

Peter was loose but not drunk. In the morning he planned to take a bus to Brownsville then walk across the border from the United States into Mexico then into the town of Matamoros. From there, he didn't know where he'd go or if he'd ever be able to go back across into his home country again.

At 2:00 a.m. the bartender rang the bell for last call and Peter considered one more shot but instead settled his bill with cash, retrieved his credit card and left the bar. The breeze off of the gulf at night had cooled the air. Peter's short sleeves weren't quite enough to keep him warm but the shock of cold air made him feel good so instead of walking directly across the street to his motel he turned left to walk a bit before going to bed.

He approached the next intersection, the streetlight blinking yellow in the late hours, and stopped for a moment to consider which way to go when he heard footsteps come up behind him and stop.

"Peter."

He froze, recognizing the voice, trying to decide whether to turn around to see the man or to run. He turned slowly.

"Good choice. Let's not make this messier than it already is," the man said.

"Gerry," Peter said. "Let's talk about this. I'll give you all the money back. I don't want anything to do with it and I won't tell anyone."

"You know it's too late for that," Gerry Howard said. His right hand came away from his side and Peter saw the pistol in his former bosses hand, the flashing yellow light behind him casting a soft reflection off the matte black surface of the gun.

"Come on, Gerry," Peter said. "What do you think you're going to do?"

"What I have to do," Gerry said.

Gerry motioned with the gun to turn left down the dark street and Peter followed his silent orders. They reached the alley that ran behind the bar Peter had been drinking in and the front end of Gerry Howard's BMW 750il sat just out of view of the main road, looking very out of place beside a trash dumpster and loading dock.

"You drive," Gerry said.

Peter climbed in the driver's seat as Gerry sat down beside him, the gun held low and out of sight but pointed at Peter at all times, Gerry's finger rested nervously on the trigger. Peter pressed the button on the dash to start the luxury German vehicle and the large engine came to life but was barely even noticeable inside the cabin.

"Where do you want me to go," Peter said.

"Take a left then head north," Gerry said.

Peter once again followed orders.

The long and narrow island moved past the tinted windows of the car on Ocean Boulevard until the motels and bars appeared less often and eventually the paved road turned to sand as they reached the furthest point of land on which the car could travel. The headlights showed only the tall sand dunes, separating the road from the beach. Peter pulled the car to a stop.

"Get out," Gerry said.

Both men exited the car and Gerry again motioned for Peter to move using the tip of the gun. They walked around the dunes until they were on the beach. The wind was much cooler now, but Peter did not notice, even in his short sleeves. His head was pounding and his bladder was putting pressure on him from the drinks earlier and the fear of dying.

Peter kept walking towards the water, his pace hurried without the intention of it doing so, until they were only a dozen feet from the surf.

"Stop there," Gerry said. "Our friends are very unhappy with you."

"They aren't my friends," Peter said. "I don't even know who they are, any names or how to contact them. If you let me go I have no information I could tell the police."

"You know enough," Gerry said. "I promised them you could be controlled. And once you proved me wrong, they need to tie up the loose ends."

"Why you? You aren't a killer, Gerry," Peter said.

"We are what we have to be," Gerry said. "It was my mistake to allow you in, so it's my responsibility to…"

"To what, Gerry. Can you even say it?" Peter said. He took small steps towards his boss, slowly to keep from being noticed.

"I know what I have to do, and so do you," Gerry said.

"Are you prepared to kill me, Gerry? Are you ready to be a murderer?" Peter said. "I've met your wife, your children. I've worked at your company for years."

"Shut up, Peter," Gerry said. "This isn't personal…"

"Of course it's personal. You're about to shoot me and that's pretty fucking personal, wouldn't you say?" Peter said.

Gerry looked down at the gun in his hand then past Peter to the surf of the Gulf of Mexico.

"I have to, Peter," Gerry said. He began to raise his arm, the gun pointing at Peter.

Peter had moved to within six feet of the man and charged him, twenty years younger and in far better shape, with the hopes he could overtake him. Gerry Howard was taken off guard by the attack and stepped backwards quickly but Peter had closed the distance and grabbed Gerry's gun hand with both of his own and raised it above their heads, pointing the barrel at the black sky above.

Gerry's finger, still on the trigger, pulled and released one of the bullets into the air. The sound brought a realness of the situation to Peter, realizing that he could soon be lying dead in the sand.

Peter released the gun with his right hand and brought a fist down into Gerry's face with enough force that it split the man's lip open and cut Peter's hand on the teeth he made contact with. Gerry flinched at the pain and with both hands pulled the gun down and into Peter's stomach but hesitated on pulling the trigger again. Peter pushed the gun aside, grabbed the barrel and turned it away from him.

They struggled in the sand, each man making advances on the other then losing ground in the position of the gun. Peter took a step to the left to take Gerry off balance but the older man was able to stay on his feet. The gun moved back and forth, Gerry never releasing his tight grip. Peter dug in with his right foot and pushed forward to topple his opponent and put all his weight towards moving the gun away from him.

Gerry Howard could tell the younger man was about to best him.

The two men were eye-to-eye on the beach, their feet dug into the wet sand as they fought each other over the gun. Peter held the slide of the pistol tightly in his hand, trying to force it into the other man's abdomen. With all his energy Gerry pushed the pistol towards Peter Miller and his forefinger pulled on the trigger.

A single Winchester 9mm bullet exited the barrel of the gun and traveled through Gerry Howard's body at 1100 feet per second, came out his back, and disappeared into the sand dune forty feet behind him. The slide flew back with the force of the gunpowder and the large spring inside pushed it back towards the front of the gun, catching the soft flesh between Peter's forefinger and thumb in between the moving parts of the gun on its way.

They faced each other motionless, the crack of the weapon between them disappeared into the dark air and all of the sounds of the beach faded away until there was nothing except a high pitched squeal in their ears from the explosion of the bullet. Peter relaxed his grip on the gun and did not notice the blood coming from him own hand where a piece of his skin was now missing. Gerry turned the pistol towards Peter and pulled the trigger but the next round had been unable to load, the flesh stuck inside the gun slowing the mechanics of the slide enough to not allow the next bullet to pull up from the magazine and into the chamber.

Gerry Howard dropped the gun into the sand and looked down at the blood soaking through his white dress shirt he'd put on that morning in his bedroom while his wife stood nearby gently applying her makeup while telling him about the day ahead of her. She was wearing the blue dress he loved to see her in and her hair flowed down over her neck and shoulders.

"I…" Gerry said. "I…"

Peter took the gun from the sand and threw it into the water then looked at Gerry.

"I'm sorry," Peter said and walked back towards the car. Before disappearing behind the dunes he turned to see his former boss once more. The man had stumbled towards the water and Peter saw him fall to his knees in the warm surf of the Gulf of Mexico and Peter wondered for a moment what the man was thinking right then.

He walked to the BMW and drove away from Gerry Howard, the dunes and South Padre Island. Not until he pulled to the side of the highway in tears half an hour later did he notice the blood coming from his hand.

CHAPTER 16

Eddie woke up in one of two beds in a motel room in Matamoros, Mexico. He could see the outline of Gus's body sitting in a chair near the door and window, his gun resting on the table in front of him. Eddie had taken first watch and they traded places at around 3:00 in the morning.

"All quiet on the western front?" Eddie asked.

"Nothing out of place. As for quiet, there are some late-night partiers that don't know when to stop," Gus replied.

Peter Miller stirred in the bed furthest from the door and asked what time it was.

"About 7:00," Gus answered. "We should get moving before too many people are up and around so we can be clear of here before getting noticed."

"Where are we going?" Peter asked.

"Austin," Gus said.

"Somehow I knew you were going to say that," Eddie said. "Do you have a plan?"

"No. I'm going to have to talk to my SAC about how we're going to handle this officially," Gus said. "I'm thinking the best place to keep Peter is in a guarded safe house."

"I feel safe with you two. Why do I have to go be babysat?" Peter said, sitting up in bed quickly.

"You confessed to killing a man," Gus turned to Peter and continued. "I'm going to get a lot of flack for not turning you in to the South Padre police department, but since your life may be in danger and your accounting of the story has it being self defense, I'm going to get you to Austin where we can protect you while we figure out how to proceed from there."

A short time later all three men were in the rented Toyota waiting in line to pass through the border patrol checkpoint to cross back into the United States at Brownsville, Texas.

"This is taking a lot longer than it should," Eddie said from the front passenger seat.

Gus rolled his window down and craned his neck through the opening to try to get a better view of what was happening a dozen cars ahead of them at the checkpoint. He quickly pulled his head back in.

"This isn't good," he said.

"What is it?" Peter said anxiously from the back seat.

"There are three black SUV's sitting in front of the station," Gus said. "And I see our friend from the Palace Bar standing in front of one of them watching the cars."

They all sat silently for a few moments to consider their situation. The van in front of them started to move forward as the border agents had cleared a car up ahead and let it cross the Rio Grande back into the United States.

"Gus, can you get us out of this line and headed back into Mexico without raising too much attention?" Eddie asked.

"I'm going to have to try," Gus answered.

He used the opening created from the minivan ahead of them moving forward to crank the steering wheel to the left and as casually as possible accelerated and made the U-turn back towards Matamoros.

Gus and Eddie had their eyes glued to the rear view mirrors and Peter had turned around completely in the back seat and they all watched the various law enforcement personnel and vehicles at the checkpoint as Gus drove them away from the border into Mexico. A man stepped out of one of the black SUV's and watched after them and raised a cell phone to his ear just as the road curved and they couldn't see the border station anymore.

Accelerating, Gus tried to put some distance between them and the river without speeding so fast as to get stopped.

"What the hell do we do now?" Eddie said.

"I'm thinking," Gus said. "I'm here unofficially so I can't technically call in for help. If State Department found out I went across the border on an extraction mission without their knowledge, I'd be screwed professionally."

"How about we leave Mexico the way I got here?" Peter Miller said from the back, still turned and looking through the rear window.

Eddie and Gus looked at each other then back at Peter.

"How did you get into Mexico?" Eddie asked.

"I flew," Peter said.

"You flew, from South Padre to Matamoros?"

"Actually from Corpus Christi, but yes. I didn't want to take any chances of my ID being logged at the crossing. So I called up and hired a plane."

"What do you think?" Eddie said to Gus.

"Well, I could do much worse than illegally avoiding passing through customs to go back into my home country, but it seems like our best chance."

Peter reached into his duffle bag and pulled out a disposable cell phone he'd bought from a shop in Matamoros and dialed.

THIRTY MILES EAST of Matamoros, the gulf lay directly ahead of them and they took the right turn onto the only road available to them. Two miles further and the road ended with no warning. Gus pushed the limitations of the Highlander SUV's off road limits and accelerated into the desert, his eyes constantly checking the rear view mirror.

"Will this actually work? Does this guy know what he's doing?" Gus asked.

"He got me here undetected. Well, until now," Peter said.

"And how did that happen?" Eddie added.

"After I shot-, after I left Gerry on the beach I took his car from the dunes but knew I couldn't keep driving it," Peter said. "So I parked it and bought the disposable cell phone and called my flying teacher, offered him money, and he gave me instructions."

They came to a stop at a deserted building surrounded by sand with the Gulf of Mexico only a few hundred yards away. Pulling up to the building a man came out, pushed open a door just wide enough for the vehicle and waved them in. Gus slowly pulled the SUV into the dark building and the door was dragged shut behind them.

They sat in dark silence for a full minute then all jumped when the man appeared at Eddie's passenger window and spoke in Spanish.

"He wants us to get out and come with him," Gus said. Eddie had understood as well, but the thicker accent and dialect slowed his own translation down.

They exited the SUV and followed the man into another room, which appeared to be the only other room, in the building. A dirty window on one side partially showed the gulf. The man began talking again with much longer sentences accompanied by hand motions towards the gulf and the building itself. Eddie struggled to keep up this time while Gus nodded his head in understanding throughout the lecture.

"He says we stay here until after nightfall," Gus said. "That it isn't safe until then."

It was only mid-morning and at least eight hours until the sun set enough to be dark out. The man left.

IT WAS JUST after midnight when the man appeared again. Gus and Eddie were wide-awake and Peter was asleep on an old sofa. They were led outside and down a trail towards the water. At the edge of a long, flat area of firmly packed sand the man stopped them by raising his hand in the air as he watched the sky out over the gulf.

A small light came on, floating out over the water and slowly getting bigger. As it grew in size the sound of a small motor became audible and louder. Minutes later the Cessna airplane touched down on the packed sand and rolled to a stop in front of them. The man went to the plane and spoke to the pilot inside the dark cockpit then returned to the three travelers and spoke in Spanish once again.

"He's asking for the money," Gus said.

Peter reached inside his bag and pulled out five large bundles of hundred-dollar bills and handed them to the man who went back to the airplane. After a minute he motioned them to climb into the plane while stuffing one of the bundles of cash into the pockets of his baggy pants.

On board the small aircraft Eddie made eye contact with the pilot.

"You never called," Eddie said to him.

"You never offered money," the pilot said. "I don't make enough giving flying lessons to locals to keep that place open."

With the three new passengers on board and strapped in, the pilot pushed the throttle forward and the plane began to move. It gained speed across the bumpy sand and took flight over the gulf of Mexico as the pilot reached down and turned off all of the airplane's lights and flipped a switch under the dashboard that disabled the transceiver, making it invisible in the dark sky. They stayed low in the air, a few dozen feet off the dark surface of the water.

CHAPTER 17

FOUR YEARS AGO

Wearing jeans and long sleeve tee shirt with a pixilated photo of Janis Joplin on the front, Eddie walked through Walter Reed Medical Center in Bethesda, Maryland. He wound through the halls, checking directions on the signs mounted at each intersection until he found the physical rehabilitation center.

He walked into the large room filled with equipment to retrain people how to walk, eat and get in and out of cars again. Three men and one woman were working with physical therapists in different parts of the room.

He looked them at each of them and knew which was the one he was looking for.

"Clem Akins?" Eddie said.

The man stood on one leg, supported by parallel bars, and paused to look at Eddie.

"Yes," Clem said.

Eddie turned to the physical therapist.

"Can we have a minute?" The therapist pulled a stool to Clem and he sat down between the two bars.

"My name is Special Agent Eddie Holland," Eddie said. He glanced around the room to see if they were in earshot of anyone else. "I'm with the Joint Terrorism Task Force out of McLean, Virginia."

Clem Akins sat staring at Eddie.

"Is that supposed to mean something to me?" Clem said.

Eddie hesitated while looking the Army Ranger Captain in the eyes.

"I was in the room," Eddie said.

Clem continued to stare at Eddie then looked away at the others getting treated then back to the FBI agent.

"That something you're really supposed to share with people?" Clem said.

"No," Eddie said. "It isn't. And you could have me removed from the JTTF and probably the FBI within the hour."

"Then why are you here?" Clem said.

"I don't really know," Eddie said. "I sat in that room and watched the operation go bad, knowing the agency didn't have proper intel, but pushed forward anyway."

"We knew that," Clem said. "They never have proper intel. They look at blurry pictures taken from eight miles up in the sky and make decisions based on that."

"Then why go in?" Eddie said. "Why lead your men in there?"

Clem laughed and shook his head.

"Because it's what we do," Clem said. "Sure, one op goes bad for every few that go right. Just because what they wanted to be in that building wasn't there, doesn't mean it was a bad operation. Normal people don't leave land mines as booby traps."

Eddie sat and thought about what the soldier said then looked at his leg and the parallel bars.

"How's recovery going?" Eddie said.

"Good as can be expected," Clem said. "Still missing a leg, but it's been a year and I'm scheduled to get fitted with one of the new prosthetics. The thing is supposed to be smarter than me."

"Would you mind if I visited again?" Eddie said.

"Don't see why not," Clem said. "It's your career."

"I'm not worried about that," Eddie said. "Only a handful of people were in that room and I bet most of them don't remember the names they saw on the screen."

"Well that makes me feel better," Clem said. "I'm glad my service was so appreciated."

"Trust me," Eddie said. "It was appreciated."

Eddie extended his hand and Clem took it.

"Maybe next time I'll break you out of here to go get a cold beer," Eddie said.

"That isn't too hard. I'm already in temporary housing down the road," Clem said.

"So what's the plan after this?" Eddie said.

"I have a few connections and if I'm lucky I won't be fully discharged," Clem said. "The Army is getting smarter and isn't automatically discharging amputees anymore if they can be a benefit. Some are even going back into combat when possible. There's a chance I'll be able to assist with training, but probably not with my Rangers."

"That would be great," Eddie said. "If there's anything I can do to help that along, I'll gladly do it."

As Eddie walked out of the building to find his car in the parking lot he pulled his personal cell phone from his pocket and dialed and he heard the operator at Fort Hood answer.

"Special Agent Eddie Holland for General Ricketts, please," Eddie said. With a short delay and one transfer a voice came from the other end.

"Eddie, how are you?" General Ricketts said.

"Doing well, sir."

"And your father?"

"Not as well, sir," Eddie said.

"That's too bad," General Ricketts said. "What can I do for you?"

"I have a favor to ask," Eddie said.

"Anything for you," General Ricketts said.

"There's a soldier sitting in Walter Reed. A Ranger," Eddie said. "He lost a leg in an operation in the sand box. I believe he'd be a great asset in training your men."

CHAPTER 18

The flight was long as they flew due east well out over the gulf before turning north to go back towards land. The pilot kept the transceiver off until they were within contact distance of Galveston, Texas. He then climbed to a few thousand feet and brought the plane back to life with lights and radio. Their invisibility cloak lifted, they headed to Port Arthur, Texas, and landed to refuel. Before departing again the pilot was met by a man on the runway and handed him another of the bundles of money to guarantee the logs showed he was alone when he landed and then took off eight hours later on a round-trip flight plan from New Braunfels to Port Arthur.

Landing just after dawn, the pilot pulled the Cessna into his hanger and got out and closed the large door before his passengers exited the airplane.

"You're on your own from here," the pilot said.

"No problem," Gus said. "We called for a ride while on the ground in Port Arthur."

The pilot shrugged as if to say 'whatever' and told them to pull the side door closed behind them as he left. They heard a car engine start and pull away.

A few minutes later another car pulled up and a horn honked a few times. They went out the side door and pulled it shut and climbed into the silver minivan that sat there idling.

"Get your asses in here, I got two kids at home wondering where I went," Shelley said from the driver's seat. They had all barely sat down when she hit the gas and headed back towards Austin.

"This is my sister, Shelley," Eddie said.

"Nice to meet you. You all are like the A-Team of Austin," Peter said, laughing. Eddie and Gus stared at him and Shelley just ignored him.

"So where to?" Shelley finally asked.

"Hyde Park," Gus said.

An hour later Shelley pulled the minivan into a driveway in the Hyde Park neighborhood of Austin. Gus got out and left them in the van and went to the front door of the house, rang the bell and waited. From the minivan they saw the door open but couldn't see who opened it. Gus stood on the porch and talked to the person inside for several minutes before finally waving to them. Eddie and Peter got out and headed to the house. Shelley backed out of the driveway and drove home.

Gus waited for them on the porch and the three of them entered the home together, Gus first, then Peter Miller, then Eddie. A tall African-American man wearing jeans and a tee shirt met them.

"This is George Silas, Special Agent in Charge at the Austin field office," Gus said.

"Pleasure to meet you, sir," Peter said.

"Please, call me George," he turned to face Eddie. "And Eddie, how are you doing? Ready to come back yet?"

"No, sir. Can't you tell I'm really enjoying my free time?"

"Yes," George laughed. "It really looks like you're taking it easy. So, Gus, I know you didn't bring these men here to chat about Eddie's extended vacation."

"No, sure didn't," Gus said. "Eddie was hired to find Peter and I'd been tasked with locating Gerry Howard, who happened to be Peter's boss."

"That's a bit of a coincidence, isn't it, both of you went missing?" George said to Peter.

"Not really," Gus said. "Turns out they were both mixed up in something. When the report came over the wire about the DB in the water in Padre, Eddie and I thought it might be one of our guys."

"Apparently it wasn't this one," George said, looking Peter up and down.

"No, but…" Gus stalled before continuing. "But he is responsible for the other one."

"And was the other one Gerry Howard?" George said.

"Yes, sir, but it's a long story. And we need your help."

The four men moved to the kitchen in the back of the house and George Silas made coffee while Peter Miller told his story.

GEORGE STOOD AT his front door and watched as Gus and Eddie escorted Peter Miller to the dark blue van that had come to pick him up and take him to a safe house. The three of them returned to the kitchen where another pot of coffee was ready.

"Everybody said I'd be bored when I told them I wanted to transfer to Austin out of the Washington Field Office five years ago," George said. "But here I am dealing with treason, murder, a communist nation and a possibly corrupt U.S. Senator."

"A senator?" Eddie said.

"The original call asking us to look into Gerry Howard," Gus said.

"You think he's involved?" Eddie said.

"Don't know. Definitely not what we see on a daily basis," Gus said. "We can't keep word from getting out about Gerry Howard's body being found. Padre PD will already have had Austin PD notify next of kin, so the senator who requested us on the case likely knows by now or will soon."

"And we don't know if the senator is involved with the Chinese or was just a friend of Gerry's," Eddie said. "But if he was involved, then Peter Miller's name will soon be mentioned to him."

"Right. So if we get pressure from above to find Peter then we'll have a better idea how big this thing is," Gus said. "And Peter never directly interacted with the senator or the Chinese."

"What are you getting at?" George asked.

"I'm thinking maybe Peter Miller goes looking to get back into the treason business."

CHAPTER 19

Eddie parked on the street in front of a gourmet pet food store then walked down the block to the gate that accesses the few dozen condominiums that were above the street level retail businesses. A man walked out and Eddie grabbed the gate and went through, looked at the signs pointing towards the various unit numbers and walked to number 211. He rang the bell and after hearing the television sound go off the door opened and Dot stood there looking at him.

"Oh my god, oh no, don't tell me!" Dot said and started crying.

"No, no," Eddie said and quickly stepped inside and closed the door behind him. "He's fine, he's alive and he's fine."

"Thank god. When I saw you I thought you were here to tell me... that he..."

"Peter is alive and well. He isn't in a position to call you yet though, and that's why I'm here," Eddie said. "Peter is in a bit of trouble and we're working on clearing it all up. Now you said nobody at work knew about the two of you?"

"Yes. Why?"

"OK. I just want to make sure you are safe, that there's no connection back to you."

"What did he do? Why wouldn't I be safe?"

"I can't get into the details right now. Just know that Peter is safe and as soon as you two can be reunited, you will be."

"Thank you so much," Dot said.

"And you can't tell anybody that Peter's back, or that you've heard from him at all. Got it?"

"Got it," Dot said.

She hugged Eddie as he left.

EDDIE DROVE ACROSS town without staying on one road for more than a mile. Watching his rear view mirror for a tail was almost taking more time than watching the cars in front of him. He got to the diner and went in and found Gus sitting in a booth.

"Dot's good and still says nobody at work knew about them, so I don't think we need to worry about her," Eddie said.

"That's good news," Gus said. "But this isn't – we got a call from D.C."

"To find Peter?"

"Yup."

"Would this be a bad time to tell you I'm heading to Rio for a while?" Eddie said.

"Yeah, it would. You are headed somewhere, though," Gus said. "I know that you left the bureau for a reason, but we need you right now and honestly, your unique position can really work in our favor."

"How's that?"

"If things go well we can claim you were working as a consultant to the field office and all of your actions were sanctioned by the SAC, which will cover your ass and cover the bureau."

"Ahh, but if it goes bad you can claim ignorance and that I was working on my own as a private detective, unlicensed at that, and protect yourselves."

"Well, I wouldn't put it quite that way, but yes, you get the idea," Gus said.

"So what's next?"

"We pack."

THE SOUTHWEST AIRLINES flight landed at Ronald Reagan International Airport in Virginia in the middle of evening rush hour. With only a carry on, Eddie purchased a Metro ticket and grabbed the next blue line train from the airport into Washington, D.C. He got off the train at the McPherson Square stop and walked four blocks to the Mayflower hotel on Connecticut Avenue and went in to the reception desk.

"How may I assist you, sir?" the young lady behind the desk asked.

"Checking in, please," Eddie said.

"Excellent, welcome to the Mayflower. May I have your name?"

"Peter Miller," Eddie said.

"Thank you, looks like we have you in a junior suite and your room is ready for you. Do you have any bags?"

"Just what I'm carrying, thanks," he said.

She handed him the keycards for his room and he signed the receipt.

He went up the elevator to the fourth floor and wound his way through the historic building until he found his room and entered with the keycard. He instinctively checked out the living room then the bedroom and bathroom.

Opening his suitcase he pulled out one suit and hung it in the closet along with the dress shirt and tie to go with it then heard a knocking from the other room. He went back into the living room and passed the door to the hallway to the one on that connected to the next guest unit and opened to see Gus standing there in an identical room.

"Sorry, I didn't order room service," Eddie said.

"You might change your mind about that," Gus walked into Eddie's suite and held up a six-pack of Fat Tire beer bottles, handed one to Eddie and sat down in one of the oversized chairs in front of the television. "Any trouble flying as Peter Miller?"

"None at all," Eddie said. "The FBI is pretty good at creating fake ID's. I guess you get to skip hotel check in altogether?"

"Can't have an Austin FBI agent check into the same hotel, or any hotel in D.C. at the exact same time as Peter Miller," Gus said. "And if the networks in D.C. are as fast as we think they are, a certain Senator already knows you're sitting here."

"As long as he doesn't know about the company I keep, then we're good," Eddie said. "So, is this actually going to work?"

"Peter says he never interacted with the senator, didn't even know about him," Gus said. "You're only four years older than Peter and travelled as him to get to DC. You're about the same size, Peter's only an inch taller."

"Now I just need to go in there and make an impression," Eddie said.

They drank their beers and talked about what they would be doing the next day. Then they talked about the FBI. Then they talked about women just like they had for twenty years, though with a bit more experience in the subject now than they'd had twenty years ago.

CHAPTER 20

Eddie was up, showered and dressed earlier than he needed, being a little more nervous than he thought he would be. Looking in the mirror, his blue pinstriped suit hung perfectly on him and his hair had grown out enough that he didn't instantly look like an FBI agent anymore. He felt naked going out without one of his hats, but he didn't have a fedora to match the suit. He grabbed his wallet full of Peter Miller's cards and his hotel keycard and closed the door behind him, went down to the lobby in the elevator and out the door to the sidewalk on Connecticut Avenue.

With a nod to the bellman a whistle was blown and a yellow and black cab pulled up. The bellman opened the cab door and Eddie got in.

"Capitol Hill, Hart Senate building, please."

Fifteen minutes later Eddie paid the cabbie and stepped to the curb and looked up at the dated 1980's office building. He walked to the entrance and emptied all of his pockets for the security line and metal detector. Once through he went to the desk and asked directions. Up the elevator and down a long taupe hallway he finally came to the door and stopped to read the nameplate affixed to the brown wood.

Senator Martin A. Barnett, Texas
United States Senate

Eddie turned the knob and walked into the room and half a dozen heads appeared above computer monitors to look at him then disappeared again, except for the nearest one.

"Yes?" asked the young woman as she looked over the top of her striped Kate Spade glasses.

"Yes, indeed. I like your positivity," Eddie said. "I'm here to see the senator."

The woman stared at Eddie for several seconds as if waiting on the punch line. When she finally realized that was the whole joke and it wasn't actually a joke she smiled an oversized condescending smile.

"Senator Barnett has no appointments this morning."

She looked to be just out of college and already had the attitude that went with working on Capitol Hill.

"Excellent, then he'll be able to see me."

"No, uh, that wasn't what I meant. He has no appointments, so you have no appointment."

"Oooh. I see the confusion here. You thought that I actually cared about what you said," Eddie said. "Now, please send word back to the senator that Peter Miller is here to see him. He'll be expecting me."

She sat with her jaw open, appalled that the man in front of her didn't see her as an authority figure.

"But, sir..."

"No 'but sir'. Peter Miller is here for the senator," Eddie raised his voice slightly, which sounded even louder than he thought it would in the small, marble walled space.

In the back of the room there was activity as an older woman quickly got up from her desk beside a large mahogany door and disappeared behind it. She emerged a few moments later and her wooden heeled shoes, though fashionable, made a loud 'clop' with every footstep as she worked her way through the maze of desks up to where Eddie stood as Peter Miller. The young girl heard the clop-clop behind her and knew what was coming and formed a smirk on her face as if to tell Eddie he'd had it now.

"Mr. Miller, I'm Ms. Evans, the senators personal assistant," she extended her hand to Eddie. "I apologize for any confusion. The senator is free and welcomes you back to his private office."

"Thank you so much, Ms. Evans, you are too kind," Eddie turned to the young lady. "I'll be sure to mention how helpful you were to the senator."

Eddie followed Ms. Evans and left the girl staring after him.

Ms. Evans led him to the mahogany door but stepped aside instead of walking in, letting Eddie pass through the frame alone. Once on the other side the door was closed behind him. The office was far less impressive than he had expected. White walls and white tiled floors made it feel more like a hospital room than a politician's office.

"You don't look like I thought you'd look," the Texas drawl made the sentence longer than it was. The senator stood from behind his large desk and walked around it to stand face to face with Eddie.

"How did you think I'd look?" Eddie asked.

The senator stood two feet from him and looked him square in the eyes for several seconds, rolling his thoughts through his mind as he rolled the stubbed end of an unlit cigar in his lips with his left forefinger and thumb.

"Weaker," the senator said.

"I'm sorry to disappoint you, Senator Barnett," Eddie said. "I could hunch over a bit if it would make me seem less imposing to you."

The senator looked at Eddie a while longer then grinned though his cigar.

"I like you," the senator said. "Gerry was a prick. You're a prick, too, but at least you're a prick with a sense of humor."

"I'll take that as a high compliment, coming from such an honorable prick," Eddie said.

"As you should," the senator turned and led them three feet to the small sitting area with a few chairs in a circle and a coffee table in the middle. "Welcome to my conference room."

They sat and Eddie poured himself a glass of water from a pitcher on the table and took a sip.

"Since you're the one sitting in front of me here in D.C. and Gerry Howard is cold and stiff in a morgue in Texas, it raises some questions, Mr. Miller," Eddie looked at the senator with a confused look for a brief moment after being called the wrong name. Realizing it he worked the look into a question.

"What kind of questions, senator?" Eddie said. "Seems like it's all pretty obvious to me."

"So it's true that you, er, took care of the late Gerry Howard?" The senator's drawl seemed to get even thicker as their discussion grew more intriguing to him.

"Senator Barnett, I trust that you aren't trying to trick me into confessing to something right here because you're secretly recording our private little conversation."

Eddie looked around the room and felt under the edge of the table as if he were looking for a recording device.

"We both have secrets that we don't want to leave this office, do we not?" Eddie said.

The senator worked the cigar around his mouth without his hands and stared at Eddie. Finally he stood and walked to the bookshelf and pulled a small digital recorder from the top of one of the hundreds of matching law books. He turned the power off then flipped it over and popped the two AA batteries out.

"I hope that was the statutes on illegal surveillance and wire-tapping," Eddie said.

The senator looked at the book the recorder had been sitting on then back at Eddie and laughed.

"Good one," the senator sat back down in his chair. "So where were we?"

"I believe we were discussing how you and Gerry Howard were partners in treason, how you ordered Gerry to kill me and how I instead overpowered him, easily I might add, and shot him with his own gun and left him for dead on a South Padre Island beach."

"Yup, that sounds like what we were talking about all right," the senator said. "So what do we do now?"

"I would never be so bold as to tell the honorable senator what his next actions should be, but I have a feeling that not only are you missing the extra income stream that you enjoyed from you little venture with Gerry, but that the source of the revenue has already put pressure on you to get your deliveries going again."

"You might be correct there, on both counts. You've been blunt with me and I'll be blunt with you. Next year is an election year and I really enjoy being a senator from the great state of Texas. These people have the ability to make sure that happens or ensure we both end up behind bars, or worse, in boxes just like the one

Gerry's headed to right now," the senator leaned forward in his seat towards Eddie. "But what do we do about your lack of employment at your former place of business?"

"That isn't a problem," Eddie said. "I have complete access to all of BaseCamp's systems. I can extract anything I want, anytime I want, and nobody there would ever know. And right now I'm sure they're all running around trying to figure out what to do after losing their fearless leader."

"When can you begin the transfers again?" the senator said.

"Is this weekend soon enough for you?" Eddie said.

CHAPTER 21

Eddie felt good as he left the senator's office thirty minutes later and chose to walk from Capitol Hill down to the World War II Memorial, where he was to meet Gus. The walk took longer than he expected, but the exercise felt good, having had to skip his morning run. As planned, Gus was waiting on a bench just across 14th Street from the memorial. Eddie took a seat beside him,

"So?" Gus said.

"So?" Eddie said. "I just came from an undercover meeting with a United States Senator where I tried to get him to admit to committing treason and all you can say is 'so'?"

"So... how'd it go?" Gus said. "Is that better?"

"Much," Eddie reached down and pulled his left pant leg up and pulled a small digital recorder from his sock and handed it to Gus. "I'm sure your boss will want to make sure this gets back into your gadget closet. But make sure to copy it first, there's some good stuff on there."

"He took the bait?"

"The senator has missed his extra income and would like it to return as soon as possible," Eddie said. "So we have some work to do."

"And you told him how to contact you, well, Peter?"

"Yup. Gave him the cell number," Eddie said.

Eddie and Gus sat and watched the tourists milling around the World War II Memorial for a while longer. Gus got up first and walked towards Independence Avenue to grab a cab. A few minutes later Eddie went the opposite direction towards Constitution and walked back to the hotel. Three hours later Eddie sat on the airplane back to Austin and slept the entire flight just as Gus did later the same evening.

The plane touched down at nine o'clock, and Eddie drove to his apartment with the stereo off. He got undressed, brushed his teeth and sat down in front of the television but never turned it on, staring at the black screen.

EDDIE WOKE EARLY and with no hesitation grabbed his running shorts and at the last moment his iPod and headed out the door. He generally preferred to run without music, but today felt that he needed something to quiet the multiple plot lines running through his head, the different ways this story he was caught up in could end.

His ear buds in, he turned on the music and got up to his pace, his footfalls coming into beat with the opening track of Spoon's 'Ga Ga Ga Ga Ga'. His chest opened wide and took in the fresh morning air, even the heat felt good to him and he moved easily. He ran for over an hour before returning to his apartment.

He left again showered and dressed in grey slacks, a loose fitting white shirt with vertical stripes, untucked and with the sleeves rolled up a couple of turns, and his charcoal twill duckbill hat with embroidered filigree on the side for a bit of flare.

He drove methodically through Austin, making many more turns than needed to make sure he wasn't being followed, and picked up Gus at his house on the west side of town. From there he continued his self-made maze through the city, across the Congress Avenue bridge, past Zilker Park and eventually to the safe house where Peter Miller was being kept.

"Hey guys!" Peter said as Eddie and Gus walked in. "Any news?"

Gus nodded to the two FBI agents who were on duty guarding Peter and they went out the back door and lit up cigarettes.

"There's been some progress but we're going to need your help," Gus said.

"Sure, anything," Peter said. "But when can I see Dot?"

"Not quite yet. We have to make sure you're out of the woods before we take any chances. She knows you're safe," Eddie said.

"Yeah, you're right," Peter said. "So what do you need? Let's get on with it."

"First off, we need to go shopping for you," Gus said.

"Shopping for what?"

"A new computer. Tell us what you need to get a secure channel open to our Chinese friends again."

"You want me to keep sending them stuff?" Peter asked.

"We need you to fake at least one, maybe two transfers to buy us some time," Eddie said. "Is that possible?"

"I actually have copies of all of the transfers I've made," Peter started writing down specs for a computer and networking equipment. "I can duplicate one and alter all of the data so at first, even second glance, it looks real. But there's no way it will hold up under deep scrutiny."

"That's fine. That's all we need," Eddie said. "We'll get everything to you today so you can set up and be ready for the first transfer in a couple days."

CHAPTER 22

Senator Martin Barnett unlocked the front door of his home in the Cleveland Park neighborhood of Washington, D.C. The large corner lot house was set on more land than the four houses around it combined and was surrounded by tall trees that sheltered the building from the street.

As he walked down the hall that ran directly through the middle of the colonial style home, he stopped at the oversized openings to each room and turned on the lights, a habit his late wife had begun and branded into Martin's psyche.

He reached the entry to his study in the back corner of the house, turned on the Tiffany lamp on his desk then went to the built in bookcase, opened a cabinet, and pulled out a bottle of bourbon and poured two fingers into a glass.

He sat down behind his desk and took a long pull on the liquor then exhaled loudly. As he pulled up to the desk and picked up the stack of papers sitting in front of him he froze as the sound of footsteps began moving slowly down the center hallway of the house.

The old wooden floorboards creaked in resistance as the steps grew louder and the owner came into view in the door.

"Mr. Xiao," the senator said. "I'd say I was surprised to see you, but of course I'm not."

"I have given you some time to think about your mistakes and I hope, for your sake, to have developed a new business plan for our joint venture," Mr. Xiao walked to the open liquor cabinet and picked up the bottle of bourbon that still sat out. "So unrefined, Senator, I would think you'd prefer something a bit smoother."

After pouring himself a short glass of the bourbon, Mr. Xiao sat in the chair across the desk from Senator Barnett and took a sip of the dark liquid.

"Like broken glass across my tongue," he said.

"It's an acquired taste," Martin took a drink from his own glass. "And yes, our plans are still in motion and you should see the next delivery very soon."

Mr. Xiao considered this new information while watching the senator closely, looking for a twitch or any other sign that he wasn't being truthful.

"I am very pleased to hear this," Mr. Xiao said. "How was this accomplished?"

"We agreed from the beginning that you would handle your end and I would manage mine," Martin said.

"You lost that privilege when the wrong man died on the beach in Texas," Mr. Xiao said. "I told you to make sure we were not compromised."

"As I said, let me manage my own business. It turns out the right man *did* die," the senator said. "Gerry Howard may have owned the company, and he indeed had some skills. But the man behind the curtain, if you will, was Peter Miller. And not only do we still have the right person working for us, it leaves more money for us. Gerry Howard was quite a demanding partner."

"You trust him?" Mr. Xiao said.

"I trust his skills, that is most certain," the senator said. "As for his loyalty, I will have that secured shortly."

The doorbell rang and both men sat still.

"Are you expecting company?" Mr. Xiao said.

"People from my office are always bringing documents by. Please excuse me for a moment."

The senator stood and walked out of the room and down the long hall to the front door and opened it. A slight man in a dark blue suit stood on the other side.

"Senator Barnett, sorry to bother you so late but the director said you would want this sooner than later," the man said and handed the senator a sealed document sized manila envelope with no markings.

The senator opened one end of the envelope with his forefinger and pulled out the several pieces of white paper and spent time looking at each page before placing them back in the envelope.

"I see," the senator said.

"Anything you need from us?"

"Yes," the senator said. "Find out who the hell that was sitting in my office yesterday morning."

He closed the door and walked back to his study to find Mr. Xiao's chair empty, the barely touched glass of bourbon sitting on the wooden table beside it. He looked down the hall towards the back door then returned to his desk and pulled out the papers that had been delivered to him and once again read the file on Peter Miller, complete with the photograph from the man's Texas state driver's license.

CHAPTER 23

Gus sat with Eddie on his favorite bench overlooking Town Lake and downtown Austin as the sun was setting. In a few minutes they would hear the screams of delight and fear from the hundred or so people lined up on the Congress Avenue Bridge to watch as several hundred thousand Mexican bats took off from their safe havens under the bridge to go out into the night sky and hunt for dinner, just as they do every night in the summer.

"George told me I'll get promoted when we finish this thing," Gus said.

"You don't sound too excited about that."

"Means I'll have to leave Austin."

"Unless George decides to leave."

Gus turned and looked at Eddie.

"You were in his home the other day. Does it look like he's planning to leave Austin?"

"True," Eddie said. "Let's finish this thing first then worry about that. Anyway, most people don't get depressed when told they're getting a promotion."

The screams began and they both looked to their right and saw the dense black cloud of bats rising from the bridge and heading east into the sky. It continued for twenty minutes before the trail of bats dwindled down to a few stragglers.

THE NEXT MORNING Eddie's VW pulled into the driveway of a large brown stucco styled house that was different from all of its neighboring houses by only the smallest details. The newly built luxury neighborhood was one of many springing up around the city and suburbs. Before Eddie could get out of his car a boy and girl came running out the front door towards him.

"Uncle Eddie! Uncle Eddie!" They screamed in unison, surely waking any neighbors who hadn't yet woken up.

As they reached Eddie each child took up position on one of his legs, their feet firmly on top of his feet and they clung on as he walked Frankenstein style.

"You two are getting a bit big for this!" Eddie said as he approached the front door where Shelley stood, leaning on the doorframe.

"If you came around more often it wouldn't be as big a show each time," Shelley said.

"I enjoy the show. If I come around more often I'd just be 'Uncle Eddie.' This way I'm always 'Uncle Eddie!'"

Once in the house Eddie sat on a footstool in the family room and turned to the kids.

"Ok. One at a time -- Sam, you first," Eddie said, and pointed at the girl and held his hands out closed into fists. "But first, how are your grades?"

"Uncle Eddie! It's summer! There's no school," Sam said.

"Oh, right, well, are you doing any summer activities or sports?"

"I'm playing tennis almost every day and coach says I'm good," Sam said. "He wants me to play in the 10 and under tournament at the end of summer."

Eddie looked up at Shelley who nodded to confirm.

"Supposedly she has the serve of a fifteen-year-old at nine," Shelley said.

"I'm almost ten, Mom!" Sam said.

"That is incredible, Sam! I'm so proud of you," Eddie said. "You make sure to have your Mom tell me when the tournament is so I can be there to cheer you on. OK. Enough delay then, pick a hand."

Sam slapped Eddie's left fist with no hesitation.

"Good choice," Eddie said as he rolled his fist over and opened his hand to reveal a small gold bracelet with a tennis racquet and ball charms hanging off of it.

Sam's mouth dropped open as she looked at it then over to her Mom and then again at the bracelet. Eddie undid the tiny clasp and hooked it to the girl's wrist. She proceeded to jump towards him and hug him so tightly he couldn't breathe.

"I love it! I love it! But how did you know?" Sam said. "I just told you I was playing tennis."

"Don't forget," Eddie said. "Uncle Eddie knows everything. It's my job."

Sam smiled and ran across the room to show her mother her new treasure. Before Eddie could say the boy's name he was standing right in the place Sam had stood.

"Shane. How about you? What are you up to this summer?" Eddie asked.

"You tell me," Shane said with a big smile.

"Ok. Let's see," Eddie looked at Shane's face then reached out and spun him around in front of him, tapping and poking him in the ribs, belly and kidneys as he turned.

"Stop it!" Shane laughed. "That tickles!"

"Well if that tickles then I'm not sure you're the big, bad blue belt in Tae Kwon Do I thought you were," Eddie said.

Shane's eyes went wide and stared at Eddie in amazement.

"How did you know?"

"Again, never doubt Uncle Eddie," He reached his remaining closed fist out and Shane slapped it. Eddie turned his hand over and slowly opened it.

Shane's eyes went even wider as he reached out and respectfully picked the item up out of his uncle's hand.

"This is a patch from my Gi. I wore it from when I began Tae Kwon Do until I earned my black belt. It's the Korean symbol for strength."

"Uncle Eddie, thank you, it's incredible," Shane said. "Can I put it on my Gi?"

"I would be honored," Eddie said.

Shane looked at Eddie then took a step backwards and brought his hands to his sides and gave his Uncle the traditional bow of respect given to your instructors and to your opponents. Eddie quickly stood up and repeated the bow to his twelve-year-old nephew.

"Now you go put that somewhere safe until your Mom can sew it on your uniform," Eddie said. Both of the kids ran down the hall, showing each other their gifts.

"You know he idolizes you already," Shelley said. "After you visit all we hear about is how he wants to be just like you."

"Maybe he should visit my apartment," Eddie said. "That might change his mind."

"Seriously, Eddie. He got into karate because of you. Fortunately he's good at it. And he's reading every book he can find in the school library about the FBI," Shelley said. "It drives his Dad crazy. He tries so hard to get Shane interested in what he does."

"No disrespect to your husband, but for a twelve-year-old to be more interested in being an FBI agent instead of an orthodontist isn't that weird," Eddie said. "Where is the doctor, anyway?"

"Samuel had an emergency call to the office. Some kid got his braces caught up in his sister's hair."

"Wow. He should have taken Shane along on that one, would have convinced him right there about the glory of being an orthodontist."

Shelley and Eddie went to the kitchen where she had been making breakfast before he arrived.

"Shouldn't be much longer," she said. "Just have to get the eggs on and make the pancakes, the batters already mixed up."

"Let me help," Eddie walked around the island and took the plastic bowl full of pancake batter from her and sprayed the griddle that was already set up on the island with non-stick spray then checked the heat by hovering his hand over the surface. As Eddie poured the first four pancakes onto the hot metal Shelley cracked and placed the same number of eggs in an oversized skillet on the stove.

"So we need to talk about Peter Miller," Eddie said as he flipped the pancakes.

"I figured as much," Shelley said. "You've been radio silent since I dropped you off in Hyde Park."

"There's been some developments and we have Peter in a safe house."

"What?" Shelley said. "How come?"

"Seems he went and killed his boss in self defense," Eddie said.

"What was his bosses name?" Shelley said.

"Gerry Howard," Eddie said.

"Holy shit, that's the senior partner's college buddy who asked us to find him."

"I figured as much," Eddie said. "Gerry Howard was into some bad things and pulled Peter Miller into the middle of it. Howard was actually trying to kill Peter, but Peter was younger and stronger."

Shelley stopped and stared at Eddie.

"That's just horrible," Shelley said. "As far as I can tell nobody at the practice knows yet."

"Happened down in Padre. We, well, the bureau has a hush order on it while we figure out what to do next," Eddie said. "But I'm sure they'll catch wind of it soon."

"I'll let you know if I hear anything."

"That would be great, help us to know if there's a leak," Eddie said.

They finished cooking and put everything on the table and the two kids came in quickly when Shelley called them. Shane sat next to Eddie and did everything he did.

Eddie left two hours later relaxed and smiling, thinking of only his niece and nephew and not of the dangerous work ahead of him. He backed out of the driveway then accelerated down the street, never noticing the green sedan parked at the curb a few doors down that had followed him there earlier that morning.

CHAPTER 24

Eddie was in bed with his eyes closed listening to his watch ticking on the nightstand and hadn't slept. He ran over in his mind the plans he and Gus had made and he thought of all the ways it could all go wrong. Once he knew sleep was not going to come, he got up and dressed in his shorts went for a run in the early morning heat.

He took his time getting ready, showered and got dressed, then made a pot of coffee and had a bowl of cereal. Once he couldn't delay anymore, he grabbed his jacket from the closet and pulled on his Cuban style cadet cap and headed out.

"Where the hell have you been?" Gus said as Eddie walked into the safe house.

"Sorry, overslept," Eddie said.

"Whatever. I hope you aren't having second thoughts about this," Gus said.

"Not at all," Eddie said. "Making plans to arrest a corrupt U.S. Senator and bring down Chinese diplomatic spies are my favorite things to do."

Gus rolled his eyes and turned his attention to the sofa where Peter Miller sat listening to them talk. His face was pale.

"You too, Peter," Gus said. "This whole plan revolves around you so you'd better suck it up and get it right."

"I know, I know," Peter said. "I'll be fine. Just thinking about what happens if I screw this up."

"Do you have the first file ready?" Eddie asked.

"Of course I do. Took me all night to prep it and make it look real," Peter said.

"So what do you do next?" Eddie said.

"I have to spoof an IP address so it masks where we are sending it from then upload the file," Peter said. "I'll bounce it through three or four different locations before it lands on their server."

"OK. Let's do it," Eddie said.

Peter went to the computer they had bought for him and quickly started typing. Within a few moments he had a command prompt on screen, bypassing the computers operating system, and was typing long series of characters and numbers. Occasionally he would stop and grunt and stare at the screen then would lean back in and furiously type again.

Twenty minutes later he got up and left the room. They heard the toilet flush then the sink run for a few seconds and Peter walked back in and collapsed onto the sofa. Eddie and Gus looked at each other then at Peter.

"So?" Gus asked.

"It's done," Peter said.

"It's done?" Gus said. "Is that it?"

"Well, I made it look like it was originating from BaseCamp. Those idiots had disabled my network login but never checked to see if I had a secondary system account," Gus said. "Then I routed a path from BaseCamp to a server in Mountain View, California, then to one in Toronto then finally Reston, Virginia, before it connected to their server in Beijing."

"Why all North American servers?" Gus asked.

"The Chinese know the file is supposed to come from the U.S. so I didn't think it made any sense bouncing around the globe, just enough to mask our true location well enough."

Eddie and Gus looked at each other again and both shrugged.

"We'll have to take your word for it. You're as much on the line here as we are," Gus said.

"Gee, thanks," Peter said.

"So what's next?" Eddie asked.

"We wait," Peter said.

"Just wait?"

"Yeah. Once the file is uploaded it's up to them to retrieve."

"How do we know they got it?" Eddie asked.

"We don't. I used to receive a phone call once a week to my cell that just meant everything was good. But I don't have that cell phone anymore."

"Well," Eddie said, turning to Gus. "That sounds like lunchtime to me."

"Sounds like a plan," Gus said.

"Can I come?" Peter asked.

"No!" Eddie and Gus said in unison as they went to the front door.

Gus opened the door and waved to the two FBI agents sitting in the unmarked Ford Crown Victoria at the curb.

"We'll be back in a couple hours to check on you," Gus said.

The two agents walked through the door. One went straight to the kitchen and started a pot of coffee while the other sat down on the couch and picked up the remote control to the television and began channel surfing.

EDDIE AND GUS sat at Magnolia Café on South Congress eating breakfast for a late lunch. Eddie was attacking a huge plate of huevos rancheros while Gus had a pair of breakfast tacos. They ate in silence, partly because the food was so good and partly contemplating the series of events they had started that day.

"A lotta ways this can go wrong," Gus spoke to himself as much as he did to Eddie.

They got back to the safe house and found Peter at his computer alternating between typing and writing notes on a pad of paper. He didn't even turn around when Eddie and Gus walked in. Eddie looked at one of the agents sitting on the sofa.

"He's been like this for thirty minutes at least," Agent Murphy said. "Just a lot of groaning and loud exhaling going on over there."

"Okay, thanks," Gus said. "Can you leave us for a while again"

"Whatever," Murphy said. He and Agent Calhoun both got up and refreshed their coffee mugs and went out to their car to sit again. Once they were gone Eddie and Gus turned their attention on Peter.

"Peter," Eddie said. "What's going on?"

"It can't be," Peter said. "I traced it before. It just can't be"

Eddie and Gus looked at each other nervously and Eddie finally grabbed Peter's shoulder and turned him around in his desk chair, away from the computer screen.

"What is going on?" Eddie said.

"It's the file packet. It got rejected," Peter said.

"What do you mean rejected, it didn't get to its destination?" Gus said.

"Exactly," Peter said. "It hit the server then a rejection came back."

"Did you try again?" Eddie asked.

"Yes," Peter said. "Same thing."

"What does that mean?" Eddie asked.

"It could mean the server is offline, either accidentally or by choice," Peter said.

Everybody was quiet for a few moments thinking about the new information.

"Why would they turn a server off when they are expecting something this important?" Gus said.

A cell phone started ringing and Eddie quickly reached into his pocket and looked at the display.

"It's him," Eddie said. Gus grabbed the television remote and turned it off, sat with Peter sat on the sofa and watched Eddie as he answered the call with the speaker on.

"This is Peter Miller," Eddie said into the phone.

"I thought we got along quite nicely in my office the other day," Martin Barnett's voice came through the tiny speaker.

"Well, I agree. Is there reason to think otherwise?" Eddie asked. "Do you not trust me to follow through on my end of the deal?"

"I cannot trust one who is dishonest with me."

The phone went dead.

"What the hell?" Gus said.

The cell phone beeped and Eddie looked at it again, his face draining of color as he did. Gus got up and stepped over to him and took the phone out of his hand and looked at the screen.

"Well," Peter said from the sofa. "What is it?"

Gus stared at the phone for a moment before he understood what he was looking at. "Only one person has the number to this cell phone, right?" Gus asked, still looking at the picture.

"Yeah," Eddie said. "I bought the disposable phone just for this."

Gus handed the phone back to Eddie and walked to the window looking out the front of the house and pulled out his Blackberry and dialed.

"George, we need a security detail dispatched immediately to the home of Samuel and Shelley Brennan, 2184 Hayes Court," Gus listened for a few seconds. "It's Eddie's sister and her kids. We have a valid threat against them."

Eddie continued to stare at the disposable cell phone's tiny screen showing a picture of him walking across a lawn with his niece and nephew standing on his feet.

"Eddie," Gus said. "This means he knows who you are." Eddie looked up at Gus then Peter then back to the phone.

"I know. But we'll have to deal with that later. Let's get them safe first then we get him."

CHAPTER 25

"You want us to leave our home?" Samuel said. "Who do you think you are, bringing my family into the middle of one of your messes-"

"Sammy, in all fairness, I got Eddie into this in the first place," Shelley interrupted her husband.

Eddie and Gus sat silently across Shelley's kitchen table from her and her husband as the couple absorbed what they had just been told.

"You're always defending him," Samuel said. "That's all you ever do is defend him and make excuses for him."

"Seriously?" Shelley said. "You want to go there? Right now? I make excuses that he can't be with his niece and nephew on their birthdays and holidays because he's working, because he has an important job."

"HAD an important job," Samuel said.

Gus looked at Eddie out of the corner of his eye to see how he was reacting to the argument taking place in front of them, but Eddie sat there calmly, having heard it all before.

"Just because he's taking a break from the bureau doesn't take anything away from what he's doing," Shelley said. "So this one case I threw his way was bigger than it looked on the surface. Can you think of anyone better to be on that job?"

"Yes, I can. Anyone else. Anyone other than someone who can bring trouble to my family, to my children," Samuel said. He abruptly stood, slamming his chair back against the wall and walked down the hall towards the kid's rooms.

Shelley watched after him then looked down at her hands, rubbing each knuckle slowly then changing hands to do the same. She spoke without looking up at Eddie or Gus.

"Can you fix this?" Shelley began to cry.

Eddie glanced at Gus who quietly stood and went down the hall to find Samuel and begin the process of moving them.

"It's what I do," Eddie said.

"Those are my kids, Eddie," Shelley said. "They're my life."

"Trust me, I understand. Those two kids and you are my blood," Eddie said. "I would and will do anything to protect the three of you."

"What about Samuel?" Shelley looked up at Eddie.

"If I have to," Eddie said. He grinned slyly and Shelley laughed through her tears.

AN HOUR LATER Gus stood at the front door talking to three different teams of agents in separate vehicles on a secure connection through his Blackberry.

"Anything from the west side?" Gus paused to wait for a response.

"All clear this way," a tinny voice came across his cell phone.

"East side?" Gus asked.

"Only car to pass in the last ten minutes was a teenager in a Honda Civic, looks clear."

"OK then. Transport?"

"We're 60 seconds out to your location. No sign of a threat and ready for pickup."

Gus turned back into the house and yelled down the hall.

"Sixty seconds out! Get your bags in here."

The family of four started appearing in the living room each carrying bags and clothes.

"When the transport arrives we'll quickly move you to the side door of the van. Leave all your bags on the front step and our agents will load them in a separate vehicle."

"Mom, what about my tournament?" Sam asked her mother.

"I'm sorry, sweetie, you're going to have to miss it," Shelley said.

A black Ford van appeared on the street and turned into the driveway then continued right onto the lawn, stopping with the side doors just outside the front door of the house. Two agents in green fatigues and bullet proof vests were quickly out of the van and standing on either side of the doors facing outward watching the two directions of the street.

"OK, time to go," Gus said and started moving the family out the door.

They each dropped their bags as they walked across the front step and climbed into the van, the kids first then Shelley then Samuel. One of the agents standing guard then climbed into the back and swung the doors shut as the other climbed into the front passenger seat and they were moving before he had his door closed. The van had been stationary less than 45 seconds.

"They gone?" Eddie came from the rear of the house where he'd been watching the backyard. He walked up behind Gus and saw the black van dropping off the front curb after cutting straight across the lawn and disappeared out of view.

"Yeah. They're gone," Gus said.

"We need to load their bags into one of the cars?"

"No. We're not sending them," Gus said. "Just help me bring them back inside."

"Don't tell me you're worried they've been bugged, are you?" Eddie said.

"Just being sure," Gus said, turning to Eddie. "They're my family, too. Plus I just wanted something to distract them while we waited on the van."

"Where they headed?" Eddie said.

"Can't tell you," Gus said.

"Good."

Eddie put his hand on Gus's shoulder for a moment then they brought in all of the bags and clothes from the front step and put them in the bedrooms then locked up the house and left.

CHAPTER 26

Senator Martin Barnett picked up his vibrating cell phone from the cup holder of his recumbent stationary bicycle in the gym of the University Club on 16th Street in Washington, D.C., three blocks from the White House.

"Yes," he said.

"The family has been picked up and relocated," a voice on the other end said.

"Do you have their location yet?" the senator said.

"Not yet, but soon. Security is tighter than usual."

"I don't want to hear from you again until you have that information for me."

"No problem, sir." The line went dead.

CHAPTER 27

It was dark in the apartment except for the dim glow of the bathroom light down the hall. Eddie didn't want to advertise he was home and had parked blocks away in Gus's cruiser and walked as cautiously as possible to the apartment building. He came from the back of the complex and through a hole in the six-foot chain link fence to keep from being seen on the street in front of the building.

He sat in the quiet darkness of his bedroom, looking down into the open drawer of his nightstand at the folded black leather wallet he hadn't carried in more than half a year. He finally reached into the drawer and picked up the three loaded magazines of ammunition that sat beside the wallet.

A short time later he left his apartment with a duffle bag full of clothes and retraced his path through the fence and back to the borrowed car.

The night air came through the open windows of the Dodge Charger as Eddie drove through Austin. Even at midnight the temperature was still in the high eighties, but it felt cooler by comparison to the heat of the daylight.

He arrived at the safe house and walked in to find Gus and Peter sitting at the small kitchen table, a half-empty bottle of Jameson's whiskey between them.

"You two getting drunk without me?" Eddie asked.

"It wasn't the intention," Gus lifted the bottle and poured into the shot glass Eddie had taken from the cabinet then topped off his own and Peter's. "It just kinda happened that way."

"At least you left some for me."

The three men raised their glasses in the air at each other then brought them to their lips and let the deep golden liquid flow down their tongues. They all sat silent for what would seem a long time to anybody not sitting at that table.

"What's next?" Peter broke the silence.

"Next, we keep drinking," Eddie said. "Then tomorrow we start phase two of our master plan."

"And what's phase two?" Peter asked.

"Hell if I know," Eddie said.

The men continued to drink until the whiskey bottle was empty then they found a few beers in the fridge. When those were done they passed out one at a time in the living room.

PETER WOKE UP last the next morning to see Eddie and Gus sitting at the kitchen table talking, Gus writing in his notepad.

"Good, you're up," Eddie said. "What would Dot be doing today?"

"Huh? What do you mean?" Peter said.

"It's Saturday morning. What would Dot usually do on a Saturday morning, if you weren't around."

"Uh, well. Let's see," Peter sat up and rubbed his eyes. "She likes to go for a manicure at a place near her condo, though once a month she has a hair appointment. Why?"

"We're going to go see her," Eddie and Gus stood and gathered their pistols and threw some food from the cabinet into a bag and headed for the door.

"What? I'm coming with you," Peter said.

"No, you're not. I didn't say we were visiting her, we're going to follow her," Eddie said. "In case the senator is having her followed to find you."

"Nobody even knows we're dating," Peter said.

"Don't get me started on that one, lover boy, we just have to be sure."

"You think Dot's in danger? I'm definitely going with you," Peter said.

"I don't think she's in danger, I just think they might be watching her."

THE DODGE CHARGER sat down the street from Dot's condo with Eddie and Gus in the front seats. The road was lined on both sides by four story buildings with shops and cafes at street level and condominiums on the top three floors. It was nine o'clock in the morning and the temperature outside was 101 degrees and without the air conditioner working hard it would be much hotter inside the black cruiser.

"If she's being followed and it's someone working for the senator, then you'd get made in a second," Gus said.

"Yeah, so looks like you're going for a walk," Eddie had on dark sunglasses and Texas Rangers baseball hat, figuring that would disguise him more than having one of his usual hats on.

Gus got out of the car and crossed to the opposite side of the street from Dot's building and casually walked down the sidewalk, stopping to look in any shop or cafe windows that wouldn't be odd for him to be looking in. He walked past the second hand kid's clothing consignment store and paused in front of the music shop with guitars, banjos and a few more than gently used fiddles in the window.

At the end of the block he crossed back to the other side and repeated the same drill, including answering a fake phone call and laughing while talking to the non-existent caller. He went into a cafe and bought a couple bagels with cream cheese and a pair of coffees then headed out to the sidewalk again.

A few minutes later he returned to the car and paused outside to watch the line of parked cars before getting in with the food and coffee.

"I like the phone call," Eddie said. "Nice touch."

"It's the details," Gus handed Eddie a coffee and the bag of bagels to take his pick. "Had to seem like a casual shopper."

"See anyone out of the ordinary?"

"Other than you, you mean?"

"Yeah, other than me."

"One guy in a green Camry, a model or two old," Gus said.

"Can't get much more invisible than a green Camry."

"Except maybe a tan Camry."

"You got me there," Eddie said. "Was this guy in the green Camry doing anything?"

"Just sitting."

"Just sitting like we're just sitting or just sitting like waiting on someone in a store?"

"Like us," Gus said. "He was outside the bagel shop. I watched him while waiting on the order. The guy barely moved his head, kept his eyes on the right side rear view."

"He's parked at the other end, facing away from the door to the apartment building?"

"Good guess," Gus said.

"I try."

They sat and ate their bagels and drank their coffee and watched the front door of the apartment building down the street in front of them.

"We want to let this guy follow her or we want to get her out of here?" Gus said.

"I'm still trying to decide," Eddie said. "I don't think he has any plans of hurting her, he just wants her to lead him to Peter. If he's even waiting for her."

"What if we give him somewhere to follow her to then?" Gus said.

Eddie looked at Gus like he was a genius and pulled the disposable cell phone from his jeans pocket and stopped dialing halfway through the number.

"If they have her line tapped then I can't give her an address or he'll just get there ahead of us to intercept," Eddie cancelled the number and dialed a new one and waited for the other end to answer. "It's Eddie, put Peter on."

After a few moments Peter came on the line and they spoke for less than a minute and hung up. Eddie redialed Dot's number and waited on her to pick up.

"Hello?" Dot said.

"Dot, it's Peter. Don't ask any questions. I just need you to meet me."

"Oh," Dot hesitated, knowing it was Eddie's voice. "Where?"

"Meet me where we first kissed."

"Uhh. OK."

"You remember where that was, don't you?" Eddie said.

"Of course I know where that was."

"OK. Go now."

Gus watched in his rear view mirror and Eddie turned around and watched out the back window. Less than a minute later they saw Dot come out the front of the building and head down the sidewalk away from them, past the green Camry and to her car parked a few spaces further down. She pulled out into the road and the Camry pulled out after letting a car pass to be in between them and Gus began to pull out to do a U-turn to follow.

"Wait," Eddie said. "Looks like we have more company."

"What do you mean," Gus was craning his head around to see what was going on just in time to see a black Suburban with tinted windows pulling out of the parking garage across from Dot's apartment building and head the same direction she had. "You think it's following them?"

"Hard to tell. Get out there now but keep a safe distance," Eddie said.

Gus got the Charger out into traffic and fell in a few cars behind the Suburban while Eddie watched further ahead.

"Dot took a right at the next light," Eddie said. "And the green Camry just turned, too."

They both watched the black SUV now to see if it would make the same turn. It approached the intersection with no turn signal then at the last second turned sharply to head the same direction as the first two cars.

"We're one marching band short of a parade here," Gus said.

"You're telling me. Now what do we do."

Gus pulled his BlackBerry out of his pocket and scrolled through his contacts while watching the road and finally clicked on a number to dial it.

"Henry, it's Gus Ramirez. I need a favor," Gus went on to explain what he needed without giving too many details to the Austin Police Department Captain then thanked him and hung up.

"Think it'll work?" Eddie said.

"Has to, doesn't it. We gotta get in front of this situation or who knows what happens to Dot."

They were coming down Guadalupe Street towards the South 1st Street Bridge when a police cruiser passed them with lights on then passed the two cars separating them from the SUV. The cruiser moved into the lane behind the Suburban and sounded the siren. After almost half a block the SUV finally braked and pulled to the right and the cruiser pulled in front of it at an angle, blocking it from speeding off.

"They won't be able to hold them off too long," Eddie said.

"Long enough for us to put them behind us," Gus said.

Gus drove past the cruiser and stopped SUV and neither he nor Eddie looked over. They sped up to catch the first two cars in their procession and got to where they could see Dot's car again.

"Think you can get there before her?" Eddie asked.

"Sure can try. We have the advantage of knowing where she's headed," Gus made a hard right turn onto a side road then turned on the flashing lights in his window once he was no longer behind the green Camry. He sped up, taking the wrong side of the road down half the street then cut left on North Lamar and turned his siren on.

"We have a couple extra miles to cover than she does going this way," Eddie said.

"She'll have to find parking on a Saturday at the park, that should give us enough time."

Most cars moved out of the way, some just didn't see or hear him in time and he passed wherever he could.

He opened the engine up as they crossed the bridge and Eddie strained to look down the water to the South 1st Street Bridge to see if he could spot Dot's car or the green Camry, but it was too far.

Once across the bridge, Gus ran the stoplight and made the hard left onto Riverside and kept his speed up until he reached the traffic circle outside the Palmer Events Center. He continued three quarters of the way around the circle then jumped the curb and came to a stop on the dry brown grass. They were both out of the car and moments later running across the park towards the water.

"We have to be ahead of them," Gus said.

"Easily," Eddie said.

They reached the other side of the park and Eddie motioned to Gus to take up position on the far side of their destination as he headed towards the trees on the side of the Stevie Ray Vaughn statue Dot would be approaching from the main parking lot and waited.

At least a dozen joggers and even more bicycles went by before he saw his first glimpse of Dot's red hair coming down the trail. She was once again wearing a sundress, green this time. He held his position and watched behind her for their mystery man from the green Camry. Dot passed Eddie without seeing him and he glanced over his shoulder and saw her go into the cutout on the trail that wraps around the statue, overlooking the water.

Looking back down the trail that came from the parking area he kept watching for the man who had taken the photograph of his niece and nephew, ready to look him in the eyes.

"Excuse me, is this the way to the Stevie Ray Vaughn statue?" a voice came from behind him. He turned to look and saw a tall man with graying hair and wide shoulders for a brief moment and then everything went black.

CHAPTER 28

Eddie was hit in the side of his skull with a black leather sap loaded with an eight-ounce lead ball and fell to the ground unconscious. The man knelt beside him and rolled his body over and reached into Eddie's back jeans pocket and pulled out his wallet.

"Eddie Holland," the man read. "Pleasure to finally meet you."

Dot came up behind the man as fast as she could run in her sundress and sandals. He heard her footfalls moments before she got to him and he stood and began to turn, bringing the sap out of his rear pocket again in one smooth motion and his striking arm out to his side to continue his swing and take her down.

Before he could she stopped just out of arms reach, raised her right arm and pulled the trigger on the canister of pepper spray from her purse, hitting the man in the face. She continued to spray until he was on his knees beside Eddie, screaming as the red pepper entered his eyes, nose and mouth.

Gus reached them at a run and Dot turned and pointed the canister at him.

"Whoa! I'm with Eddie," and held out his badge in its folding black wallet. Dot dropped the pepper spray to the ground and fell to her knees and watched as Gus pushed the man onto his stomach and placed handcuffs around each wrist and tightened them as far as they would go

"Why did he attack Eddie? What's going on?" Dot said.

"He's trying to find Peter," Gus said.

"And you used me as bait?" Dot said.

"Well, yeah," Gus said.

"Cool," Dot said.

Gus helped her up from her knees and pulled out his phone and made a call.

Two ambulances, half a dozen Austin police cruisers, and a pair of cars from the FBI field office were parked on the dead grass of the park surrounding him when Eddie came to. The paramedics had him on a stretcher and had placed a c-collar around his neck as a precaution and were checking his vitals.

"What the hell happened?" Eddie said, looking around at Gus and Dot.

"That happened," Gus pointed at the man with handcuffs and ankle shackles on as a pair of medics were rinsing his eyes with water.

"And what happened to him?"

"I did," Dot said.

Eddie looked at the man being treated and back at Dot.

"Good job," he said.

"Thanks," she smiled.

Eddie reached up and fumbled with the c-collar to remove it from his neck as the paramedic argued with him to keep it on 'for his own safety,' but Eddie won.

"You're going to be sore for a few days, sir," the paramedic said.

"No shit," Eddie said and turned his attention back to the man who had struck him.

"You get anything out of him yet," Eddie asked Gus.

"Right now the answer to every question is 'go fuck yourself.' Just waiting on the paramedics to finish with him so I can press a little harder."

Eddie turned and dropped his legs off the side of the stretcher and stood up then fell to his knees. The paramedic took one arm as Gus grabbed the other and they sat him back on the stretcher.

"Not so quickly," the paramedic said. "You may have won the c-collar battle but we're still taking you for an MRI to make sure you don't have a concussion."

Eddie turned and looked at Gus who just nodded as if to say "don't fight it, just go with them."

"Dot," Gus said. "Looks like you're gonna get to see your guy."

"Really?" Dot said.

"Well, after this I think it would be safer for you to join him under our protection," Gus said.

"Take me to him now!"

The ambulance left with Eddie while Gus took Dot to the safe house and another agent took Dot's car to the field office to be kept until she could retrieve it.

CHAPTER 29

Senator Barnett sat in the back of a white Lincoln SUV as it pulled through the gate to the business jet runway at Dulles Airport in Virginia. He reached into the left breast pocket of his suit jacket and pulled out his vibrating cell phone and read the message on the screen.

Smiling, he forwarded the information he'd received to another number, closed the phone and climbed out of the vehicle and boarded his private airplane as two staff members retrieved his luggage from the trunk and placed it on the aircraft.

After a short wait for two other airplanes to depart, the Hawker 4000 climbed to 36,000 feet as it headed southwest towards Austin, Texas.

CHAPTER 30

"We know who hired you," Gus said. "Just want to hear you say it."

"Go fuck yourself," the man said once again.

Gus picked up the man's wallet and started pulling everything out and dropping it on the table after inspecting each piece.

"Aston Marshall," Gus read from the man's driver's license and laughed. "Seriously? Aston? A heavy named Aston?"

"Go fu-"

"I know, I know. Go fuck myself," Gus said. "You should really learn a few more phrases, Aston."

Gus laughed out loud again.

"I don't know if I can even brag about catching a guy named 'Aston'. I may just have to pass it off to some rookie agent to claim the collar."

Aston Marshall stared at Gus, his hands cuffed to the steel bar in the middle of the table and his feet shackled to a steel ring mounted in the floor.

"Why don't you unlock these cuffs and you'll see how tough someone named Aston can be."

"As intriguing as that sounds… no," Gus said. "First of all you're fifteen years older than me so it would just add that much more embarrassment if I not only arrested an old man named Aston but beat him up as well."

"Fu-"

"Seriously, you really need to expand your vocabulary," Gus said. "Wait a second, what do we have here?"

Gus dug into the wallet and pulled a business card out that had been shoved into the worn out lining of the interior pocket.

"Senator Martin Barnett," Gus read. "You actually have the business card of the man who hired you in your wallet. Do you have the cancelled check he paid you with in here also?"

As Gus continued to look through the wallet a beep came from the grey plastic container that held all of the personal items the man had on him when he attacked Eddie.

"Looks like you're getting a text message, Aston," Gus said. "Let me check that for you."

Gus reached into the container and pulled out the small phone, tapped a button on the keyboard and read the message to himself twice, the second time recognizing it as the address Samuel, Shelley, Sam and Shane Brennan were being safeguarded.

"Can you tell me how it's possible that confidential FBI information is being texted to you?" Gus said.

"I want a lawyer," Aston Marshall said.

"I bet you do."

Gus gathered all of personal items into the grey container and left the man cuffed to the table in the small interrogation room. Down the hall he stepped into his boss's office, closed the door behind him and handed him the cell phone.

"Looks like we have a leak," Gus said.

George Silas read the message on the phone and handed it back to his agent. He turned his chair and looked out the window overlooking downtown Austin and the state capital building in the distance.

"It's a good thing they never made it to that house," George said.

"Excuse me?" Gus said.

George turned back and looked at Gus.

"The Brennan family is safe and secure," George said. "With the powers involved in this I wanted to be certain of that."

"You suspected a leak?"

"I didn't so much as suspect one as I expected one," George said. "We need to watch our every step until this is over."

CHAPTER 31

Gus parked in front of the emergency entrance to the hospital, flipped the passenger side sun visor down to show the blue and white lights clipped to it and went to find Eddie. After poking his head behind three different curtains he found him sitting up on a bed, his shirt off and several electrodes stuck to his bare chest as a monitor beeped out a steady rhythm beside him.

"Where the hell have you been?" Eddie said.

"Questioning your new best friend."

"And?"

"He lawyered up right after I found this in his wallet," Gus handed Eddie a sealed evidence baggie containing the senator's business card.

"You can't be serious?" Eddie said. "He had this on him?"

"Sure did," Gus said. "We have him at the field office to keep it quiet, don't want the senator finding out we've snatched him."

Gus pulled the curtain back and looked both ways and then closed it again and turned to Eddie.

"While I was in there with him, he got a text message," Gus said. "It was the address where we sent your family."

Eddie jumped up and reached to pull the wires from his chest.

"Wait, it's OK," Gus said. "They never went to that house. George wanted to be extra cautious and rerouted them. He didn't tell anybody and hand-picked the agents who moved them."

"He used them to flush out a leak?" Eddie said.

"Well, you could put it that way," Gus said. "I like to think that he was protecting our own."

A doctor in a long, white lab coat came through the break in the curtain, her brown hair pulled back and she looked tired. She glanced at the monitor, then pulled out the long feed of white paper that had been gathering in a basket below the screen. After a minute of scrolling through and marking a few points with her ballpoint pen she looked at Eddie for the first time.

"I'm Dr. Taylor," she said. "The MRI came back and everything looks normal, we can get you released and out of here shortly, but I want you to follow up with your primary physician in a week."

"Well, thanks, Doc," Eddie said. "Happy to hear it."

"I'd recommend no excessive physical labor or exercise for a few days and ibuprofen for any pain."

"What about running?" Eddie said.

"Wouldn't recommend it," the doctor made notes in Eddie's chart.

"Mountain climbing?"

"Definitely not."

"Quiet dinner for two?"

"That would be fine."

"Great. Next Saturday night, 8:00?"

The doctor paused and looked up from the clipboard at Eddie.

"Excuse me?"

"I asked you if you'd like to go for a quiet dinner for two and you said that would be fine," Eddie said.

"Should I pick you up here at the hospital or somewhere else."

She stared at Eddie to see if he was being serious but nothing about his expression made her think he wasn't.

"We aren't allowed to date patients," Dr. Taylor said.

"You were barely my doctor. The guy who treated me the last three hours was an old man who looks like Ernest Borgnine. And he turned my dinner invitation down anyway. You merely checked my heart monitor and signed my discharge."

"That's not the point, Mr…"

"It's, what, 3:15 right now," Eddie glanced at his wristwatch. "So you just came on for the evening shift and inherited me from Dr. Borgnine. I've had longer interactions with toll booth attendants than I've had with you, so… were you really my doctor?"

"And how many toll booth attendants have you asked out?" she said.

"Three," Eddie said. "And only one said yes."

The doctor laughed and shook her head at him and turned to Gus. "Is he always like this?"

"I've known him most of my life and have never seen him like this," Gus said.

"So, Mr. Holland," she said, "should I take this as a great compliment that you asked me out or as a symptom of a concussion the MRI missed? With a stroke of this pen I can have you wheeled back upstairs for so many tests that your insurance company will send you a get well card."

"Maybe being hit in the head has made me realize how short life is. I could walk out that door and get hit in the head. Again. Though that's highly unlikely. I'm usually a bit quicker than that."

"That's true," Gus said. "He usually is a lot faster. He's just getting old."

"Not helping, Gus," Eddie said. "So, how about it Doc?"

"Mr. Holland," Dr. Taylor said. "I've been here since 3:00 yesterday afternoon and have had no more than thirty minutes of sleep. I've also been hit on by no less than half a dozen men and one woman in that time. So as cute as you think you're being, you're just another stack of paperwork I'll have to complete before I ever get to go home and get some real sleep."

"OK, I didn't want to do this, but my friend here has a gun and has been known to use it on women and children," Eddie said.

"It's true," Gus said, pulling back his sports coat to expose his holstered pistol and his FBI badge clipped to his belt. "Except for the part about children. I would never shoot a child."

"But you would shoot a woman?" she said.

"Oh, hell yes," Gus said.

"Well, as honored as I am," Dr. Taylor said, "I still have to say no."

CHAPTER 32

Eddie slept soundly after laying awake thinking about Peter Miller, the senator, and the Chinese. The pounding in his head had reduced from thunderous to thudding. He was glad to be back in his apartment with Aston Marshall locked up.

Just before sunrise a beeping sound stirred him and he reached out to turn his alarm clock off but the sound kept going. He realized it was the disposable cell phone and climbed out of bed and found it in his jeans pocket from the night before.

"Hel-," Gus cut him off.

"Get dressed and to your curb right now, I'll be there in less than a minute."

Eddie could hear the siren on Gus's cruiser through the earpiece and before he could reply Gus had hung up. As Eddie began to pull his jeans on he heard the siren coming down his street and he hurried to get his sneakers on and grabbed a T-shirt, a hat and his gun while rushing out the door. He ran down the stairs and through the courtyard as Gus screeched to a halt in front of him, his front right tire jumping the curb. Eddie was barely in the car when Gus accelerated, causing the passenger door to slam shut.

"Fill me in," Eddie said, pulling his T-shirt on and clipping the gun's holster to his belt.

"It isn't good," Gus said, taking the next left through a red light at speed. "Aston Marshall is loose."

"How the hell did that happen?"

"Middle of the night, rookie agent is at the call desk and two lawyers in thousand dollar suits walk in with a signed order from Judge Cartwright to release him," Gus said.

"Shit. The senator must have found out and used one of his local cronies to free him."

"That isn't the worst news. I can't get an answer at Peter's safe house, neither agent's phone is getting picked up," Gus said.

Eddie pulled his Glock 23 out of its holster, keeping the barrel pointed to the floorboard, and released the magazine to confirm it was fully loaded with 15 rounds. He clicked the magazine back in place with his palm and pulled the slide back to check the 16th round resting in the chamber and kept the weapon out of its holster.

"Have you called in support yet?" Eddie said.

"Got off the phone with George right before calling you or I'd have given you at least another minute's notice," Gus said. "FBI SWAT team is assembling and scrambling but we're still a good ten minutes ahead of them."

"And we aren't waiting for them, I gather," Eddie said.

Gus glanced at Eddie and back at the road then reached up and turned the siren off as he made the hard right onto the safe house's street.

"I'll take the back door," Eddie said.

"Works for me."

Gus brought the cruiser to a hard stop in front of the house and both men were out and moving, pistols drawn and angled towards the ground in front of them as they ran towards the house. When they reached the front corner Eddie looked at Gus.

"Ten count," he mouthed then rolled to his left and worked his way to the rear of the building while Gus took the five wooden steps up the front porch of the house slowly, keeping count in his head. When he reached 'ten' he pushed away from the front wall and turned. With a single kick to the door it swung open and slammed against the wall and he heard the back door do the same thing a half second later.

They worked towards each other through the house to clear the rooms, guns raised, fingers resting on the trigger guards. Neither stopped as they each found blood splatter on the back of the sofa in the living room and across the refrigerator in the kitchen. They met at the kitchen door then moved silently down the dark hallway to the two bedrooms.

Both men saw the pool of blood on the carpet outside the bedroom doors and looked at each other to confirm.

Gus motioned for Eddie to take the left bedroom door and he'd take the right. When in position, they both turned the knobs and pushed through the doors with their shoulders and stepped into the two rooms at the same time.

Eddie moved in, quickly keeping his back to the wall and before he could get a full scan of the room, a gunshot sounded from the next room, the bullet coming through the wall just past his right ear. He dropped to the floor and began to move out of the room in a crawl and got to hallway.

"GUS!"

"I'm good," Gus said. "We're good."

Eddie leaned left and looked over his shoulder into the room to see Gus squatted down just inside the door at the foot of one of two twin beds in the room, gun raised and aimed at Dot who was hiding behind the headboard of the other twin bed. A gun was on the floor in front of her.

"Are we good now, Dot?" Gus said calmly.

"Yes," her voice trembled and she began to cry. "I thought you were him again. Coming back to kill me."

Eddie was on his feet and moved into the room, gun still raised and pointed at Dot as he cautiously moved towards her, put his left foot on the gun, and kicked it back to Gus. Eddie holstered his weapon and helped Dot to her feet and turned her around to face the wall. Gus patted her down from top to bottom to check for other weapons.

"Why are you doing this to me!" Dot said.

"You shot at a federal agent. I have to," Gus said to Dot after turning her back around. "Where's Peter? Where's the agents?"

She began to cry and pointed to the other side of the room and they turned and saw Peter Miller for the first time that day. His body was curled up across from where Dot had hidden, behind the headboard of the other bed, a pool of blood under his left arm.

Gus reached for his phone and pressed the two buttons to get him connected the SWAT team that would be there momentarily and Eddie stepped over, knelt down and pressed two fingers to the carotid artery in Peter Miller's neck.

"We had one shot fired by a friendly upon entrance with no contact. One person already down on arrival. Have not located the agen-"

"Gus, he's alive," Eddie cut Gus's report short. "Get an ambulance here, now."

"Correction we have one person shot with a pulse. Need medical support pronto." Gus hung the phone up and stepped over to Dot. "Where are the agents?"

Dot looked at the closet door then back at Gus and slowly shook her head as she lowered her chin.

Gus stepped to the closet door and slowly pulled it open then dropped to his knees. The two agents sat side-by-side in the closet, a black hole in the middle of each of their foreheads and blood soaking through their shirts where bullets had entered their chests.

Eddie came over and put his hand on Gus's shoulder. The sirens of the SWAT team's vehicles began to come through the windows and got louder as they approached the house. An urban assault vehicle with six FBI SWAT agents in full armor jumped the curb and stopped at the porch. Within half a minute the team was through the house and at the bedroom.

"Clear the way," a booming voice came from behind them and George Silas stepped through the door. Eddie stepped back and George knelt down beside Gus and looked at the two dead agents in the closet.

CHAPTER 33

"Peter was in the bed by the door and I was in the other one, we were both sleeping," Dot began to tell Gus and Eddie what had happened in the half hour before they got to the safe house.

"You were in separate beds? There's a double bed in the other room," Eddie said.

Dot blushed. "Oh, Peter and I have never slept in the same bed together. We don't, well, I've never…"

"So when you'd stay at his house?" Eddie said.

"Guest room."

"And all your trips to the gulf?"

"Separate beds."

"OK, then. Go on."

"Well, we were asleep and a loud cracking sound woke me up. I looked over and Peter had sat up and was motioning for me to be quiet. We heard the noise again and realized it was a gun."

"And this was coming from the other room, the living room?" Gus said.

"Right, well, that's what it sounded like at least," Dot said. "Peter whispered to hide so we both got out and hid at the ends of the beds. It was really quiet in the other room then the door slammed open against the wall and that guy, the one from the park, came in with a gun. Then Peter, I don't know why he did this, he tried to push his bed real fast into him, to knock him down. But the bed didn't slide as easily as he thought it would. And when he stood up to push it, Aston shot him. And he fell where you found him."

Dot started crying, "I thought he was dead. When can we go to the hospital?"

"Soon. We just need to get the rest of the story first," Gus said. "Can you do that?"

"OK. I can do that," she wiped underneath both of her eyes with the bottom edge of her hands. "I screamed when Peter fell to the floor so he knew I was there. He walked over and looked down at me and pointed the gun at me for a long time. Then he went and dragged the first of the two agents in here. He was walking back out to get the other one and his phone rang."

"He answered a phone call?" Eddie said.

"Yes. That's when I crawled over and took the agent's gun," Dot said.

"You did what?" Eddie said.

"I knew he was going to kill me, especially after I pepper sprayed him in the park."

Eddie and Gus looked at each other and back at Dot waiting for the conclusion of the story.

"After he hung up he pulled the other agent in and put him in the closet, then he shot each of them in the chest."

"Were either of the agents moving or making sounds? Why did he shoot them again?" Eddie said.

"I don't know. I really don't know," Dot said. "That's when he turned back to me and I was already standing with the gun pointed at him. He just smiled at me and began to raise his gun."

She started crying heavily, searching in her purse for an unused tissue. Once she had stifled the tears she continued.

"I hesitated. I've never shot anyone. I'd never even held a gun before. It's like he knew that, could sense that, and he pointed his gun at me," she said. "Then I shot him."

"You shot him?" Eddie said.

"Yes. It hit his shoulder… his right shoulder. He fell backwards into the hallway," Dot said. "I stayed there for what seemed a long time, it was probably only seconds, with the gun pointed at his body on the floor. Then I ran over and slammed the bedroom door closed and went to Peter."

"And what happened to the man?" Gus said.

"I heard the siren coming," Dot said. "And then I heard him get up then heard the back door slam."

"We barely missed him," Eddie said.

EDDIE DROVE DOT to the hospital and Gus stayed at the safe house searching the bedroom with George Silas. The two agent's bodies had been placed on stretchers and removed after Gus and George took a look at the bullet wounds in their chests and foreheads.

"Gus, we have a through and through on Calhoun here," George said. He had Agent Calhoun's body raised on it's side with the help of the medical examiner and was inspecting the torso.

206

Gus looked up at George then into the back of the closet. He took his flashlight off his belt and squatted down, avoiding the two pools of blood. In the back right of the dark closet behind where Agent Calhoun had been Gus found the small hole in the wood. He pulled his pocketknife out and dug into the hole with the opened blade and pulled out the compacted bullet that had traveled between the agent's ribs, through his heart and out his back into the wall.

"Looks like a .38," Gus said.

"Bag it," George said. "We pulled the round out of the wall in the other bedroom from the shot she fired at you, it was a .40."

"Makes sense, she was using Calhoun's P229. Where is it?"

"In the other room, the forensics guys are clearing it."

Gus walked to the living room and found two pistols and a revolver lying on a cloth on the coffee table where a forensics officer was retrieving fingerprints, photographing the weapons then removing the magazines and ammo and logging the number of fired rounds.

"What do we have here?" Gus said.

"The Glock 23 on the left was Agent Murphy's, found one set of prints and a full magazine, one in the chamber," the agent said. "The Sig P229 .40 cal was Agent Calhoun's. Found two sets of prints and three rounds have be fired."

Gus took notes as he listened.

"All three casings are accounted for from the bedroom," the agent said. "And the .38 Smith & Wesson was presumably the perp's that he brought with him. Hired hitters sometimes prefer revolvers to avoid any casings being left behind. Four shots fired, two left in the cylinder."

"Four? Are you sure?" Gus said.

"Yes," the officer said. "Basic math. Six minus four equals two. The spent casings are still in the cylinder and all test positive for having been fired recently."

"Thanks," Gus walked back into the bedroom. "We have seven shots fired, Calhoun's pistol got off three rounds."

"And both agents tested negative for fresh gunshot residue, so he didn't pull the trigger," George said.

"Right, and Marshall's .38 fired four rounds which accounts for the double shots on Calhoun and Murphy," Gus said. "Dot said she picked up Calhoun's Sig and shot Marshall, then the round through the wall that almost got Eddie. What about Peter Miller then?"

"Get back with her tomorrow," George said. "She just went through a pretty traumatic experience, probably was just confused."

PETER MILLER WAS taken straight through the emergency room and up to the third floor for surgery. Dot and Eddie sat in the waiting area staring at the beige walls while a small flat screen television hanging from the ceiling showed CNN with the volume off. It was nearly four hours before word came from the operating room.

"Agent Holland?" A doctor approached them. He still had his surgical cap on and his mask was down over his throat.

"Yes," Eddie stood up and Dot sat up straight behind him in her chair.

"He's one lucky man, I have to say. The bullet missed his heart by less than ten millimeters. It did do some major damage on the way through, but nothing we weren't able to fix."

"So he's OK?" Dot asked from her seat.

"He's out of surgery and he's stable in recovery. It's still going to be a long road back for him, but he should be fine. A man in any less shape wouldn't have fared as well."

"When can we see him, Doc?" Eddie said.

"He'll be in recovery for a few hours, then if he's still stable he'll move to a room and you can see him. But I can't promise he'll even know you're there; with injuries like his, we have to keep him well sedated to insure he doesn't do anymore damage. Could be a couple days before he's really alert enough to talk."

"I understand. Thanks," Eddie said. The doctor turned and walked back down the hallway.

"So, do you feel a bit better? Sounds like Peter will be just fine in time."

"Just a bit," Dot said. "Would feel a whole lot better if I could see him."

"Soon enough, but for now let's get you something to eat. We've been sitting here for hours."

Eddie and Dot walked to the cafeteria, the first time Dot had left the waiting area. They ate then sat and drank several refills of coffee, waiting until they could get in to see Peter. They returned to the waiting area after a few hours and asked the nurse at the desk if they would be able to visit him yet.

The nurse directed them to Peter's room where they found him sleeping, his face pale behind the oxygen mask covering his nose and mouth. The whirring of the machines filled the otherwise quiet room. Dot sat beside

Peter, watching him sleep. They spent an hour in silence before Eddie took Dot out of the room.

"We can come back tomorrow, you need rest. We've arranged a hotel room for you. Agents will be in the room next door," Eddie said.

Dot nodded and they left the hospital and Eddie drove to the hotel and introduced her to the agents who would be watching out for her.

"I'll come by in the morning to get you and we'll go back to the hospital," Eddie said.

"Okay. Thanks," Dot said and retreated into her room. Eddie went back to the room next to hers.

"Everything set up, guys?" Eddie said to the two agents. They sat at the small table in the hotel room where they had several monitors showing streaming color video of the hallway outside the room, outside the elevator and stairwells down the hall, and the main lobby.

"All set, Eddie," one of the agents said. "We'll let you know if we need you."

CHAPTER 34

George Silas sat alone in his living room and watched a baseball game on television, the Texas Rangers hosting the New York Yankees and New York was up by three runs. Derek Jeter fielded a low bouncing ball and had it thrown to first base before the runner could touch, ending the fourth inning. George groaned and swore at Jeter under his breath and stood. With his wife out of town to keep him from having caffeine too late, he walked into the kitchen get another cup of coffee.

Jean Silas was used to her husband never taking vacations and had begun to travel on her own or with her friends. Currently she was in Seattle with three women she regularly played tennis with at the country club. George hated her traveling without him, but never seemed to find the opportunity to take time off.

The coffee maker heated the water George poured in the top as it worked down through the hand ground beans and into the mug that waited to receive it. As the mug began to fill a hand knocked on the back door to the house a few feet from him. He glanced at his watch and stepped to the door and opened it as he flipped the outside light on.

The barrel of a gun came through the doorway and George stepped back as two Chinese men he did not know entered his home. The man with the gun was tall and wide and wore all black. The heavy HK45 pistol was held firmly in the air and stayed pointed at George. Mr. Xiao stood beside him and wore a black suit with a white shirt and a purple tie and had the air of being in charge.

"What do you want?" George said. "Who the hell are you?"

"We are concerned citizens," the small man said. "And we have a simple request for you that I am sure you will choose to comply with."

"OK," George said. "Just put the gun away and we'll talk."

"I'm afraid I would feel more comfortable if my colleague kept his weapon on you," Mr. Xiao said.

"What is it you want?"

"We simply need you to make two phone calls and relieve your agents of their post at the hotel and the city police officers at the hospital," Mr. Xiao said.

"You know I can't do that," George said. "It's my job to make sure those two individuals are protected."

"Such bravado," Mr. Xiao said. "Impressive but confusing. You do not even know these two people."

"It doesn't matter, they're in my protection."

"Very well," Mr. Xiao said. "I didn't wish to do this, but you leave me no choice."

The small man glanced down the hallway and with a smile stepped out of sight then returned with the Louisville Slugger baseball bat with Nolan Ryan's signature that George had hanging on the wall next to his other baseball memorabilia.

"Your wife is staying at the Olympia Hotel in Seattle in room 728," Mr. Xiao said. "This morning she had room service delivered, two eggs with toast and an orange juice."

"What?" George said. "What are you talking about? How do you know that?"

"Our reach goes well beyond Austin, Special Agent Silas," Mr. Xiao said. "And now back to our request, if you would be so kind to make the phone calls we ask of you then no harm will come of your wife. She won't even know she's been watched the last three days."

"You son-of-a-bitch," George said. He sized up the big man but the bodyguard only grinned and raised the pistol a little higher.

Mr. Xiao stepped to the large man and handed him the baseball bat and took the gun from him, keeping it aimed at George.

"Now, those phone calls?"

George hesitated, then pulled his Blackberry from his pocket and dialed the agent at the hotel where Dot was staying.

"It's George," he said. "Everything is clear, you and your team can pack up and head home." A short conversation later with very few details and George hung up. He dialed his contact at the Austin police department next and told him he could pull his officers from guarding Peter Miller at the hospital.

"There," George said. "It's done. Now forget anything you know about my wife and get the hell out of my house."

"Very well, Agent Silas," Mr. Xiao nodded his head at the agent, lowered the gun then turned and walked out the back door. The large man raised the autographed baseball bat and before George could lift his arms to defend himself brought it down into his skull.

George fell to the floor, his head caved in and blood streaming from his nose. The big man knelt down and checked his pulse and felt for air coming out of his nose. Once satisfied, he stood and walked out the door, throwing the bat on the floor.

CHAPTER 35

Eddie left the hotel and drove to the FBI field office and was buzzed in. Down the hall he found Gus sitting at his desk.

"What's going on?" Eddie asked.

"Just got word that the bullet they pulled out of Peter's chest was a .40 caliber," Gus said.

"Dot said that Marshall shot Peter with the gun he brought with him, the .38," Eddie said.

"Exactly."

"Could she be confused? Maybe Marshall picked up Calhoun's Sig and used it," Eddie said.

"But why would he do that, he had two rounds left in his Colt," Gus said. "Plus, his prints weren't on it."

They sat quiet, both rolling the math and logistics of guns and bullets through their heads.

"Where's Dot now?" Gus said.

"Why, you don't think…" Eddie said. "Why would she shoot her own boyfriend?"

Gus sat up in his chair and pulled the keyboard to his computer closer to him and did a search for Dorothy Jeffries.

"She's clean," Gus said. "No record except for one speeding ticket in San Antonio last year."

"Try Facebook," Eddie said.

Gus pulled up the social networking site and logged in as the fake user that he used to search the site and typed in Dot's name and soon had her profile on screen.

"She doesn't even have her profile blocked from non-friends," Gus said.

"She has over 300 friends," Eddie said. "Scroll through them.

Gus clicked on Dot's friend list and began scrolling slowly down the list of names and thumbnails of their faces, pets, babies and whatever other images they'd used as their profile pictures.

"Stop there," Eddie said.

"What do you see?" Gus said.

"Alicia Howard, Ian Howard, Maggie Howard …" Eddie read from the list.

"You think they're related to Gerry Howard?" Gus said.

"Either that or it's a huge coincidence," Eddie said. "See if we can get any info on them."

Gus clicked each name then back to Dot's list.

"They all have privacy set on their accounts," Gus said.

"Just like the family of a man who runs a government contracting company would," Eddie said. "So how do we find out if they're related?"

Gus typed Ian Howard's name into the search bar in Facebook and several dozen results came up. He scanned down the list until he saw the same profile picture from Dot's friend list.

"Here he is," Gus said. "Ian Howard is from Austin. His profile may be locked but luckily for us it shows where you're from when you're searching."

"Run his name," Eddie said.

Gus switched back to the FBI's system and searched for Ian Howard and found him.

"Here he is," Gus said. "Twenty-one years old, lives in an apartment by the university, probably a student."

"Look there," Eddie said, pointing further down on the screen. "His previous address, most likely his parents house."

Gus took the address and did a reverse search and came up with the home's primary resident's names and leaned back in his chair.

"Gerald and Leigh Howard," Gus said. "I'll ask again. Where did you say Dot is?"

EDDIE AND GUS were in the black Charger headed for the hotel Dot was put up in and Eddie was calling the agents in the next room.

"Agent Harris," a voice came from the other end of the line.

"It's Eddie. Is she still in her room?"

"What are you talking about," the agent said. "We were called and told to pack up three hours ago. I'm at home in bed."

Eddie turned to Gus. "Drive faster."

"Who called you?" Eddie said into the telephone.

"Well, George did," the agent said. Eddie sat silent then thanked him, hung up and dialed George Silas's cell phone number.

"This isn't good," Eddie said. "Ben said that George called and ordered them to stand down, there's no security on Dot."

"What?" Gus said. "Why would he do that?"

"I don't know, but there's no answer on his cell," Eddie said.

"You think another call from DC?" Gus said.

"I think George would have called us first before giving the stand-down to let us get over there first."

Gus had his blue lights and siren on and went through two red lights then took a left on a third red and pulled into the circle drive of the hotel on the south side of the city near the chain restaurants and box stores.

Once in the lobby, Eddie went for the elevators and Gus stopped to get the manager. Eddie got to Dot's door on the third floor and knocked loudly and tried the locked doorknob. Gus and the hotel manager came off of the elevator and over to the room door.

"Open it," Eddie said.

"I can't without-" the manager began to talk.

Gus had his badge out and in the manager's face.

"I know the old life-or-death line is a bit overdone, but this is life-or-death," Gus said.

The manager looked at the badge then pulled his master key from his pocket and opened the door. Eddie pushed in as soon as the lock clicked and Gus followed.

"She's not here," Eddie said.

"No suitcase and nothing in the bathroom," Gus said. "Doesn't look like she was coming back either."

They rushed past the manager and ran to the door to the stairs, down to the lobby and out to Gus's car and sped away from the hotel. Eddie called the hospital and got through to the nurse's station on Peter Miller's floor.

"This is Eddie Holland," he said. "With the FBI. Is there still a police officer outside room 419, Peter Miller's room?"

"No, I don't believe so," the voice came through. "I saw him leave a few hours ago."

"I need you to call hospital security and get them there immediately," Eddie said. "I'll be there in three minutes."

Eddie hung up the phone as Gus turned into the drive to the main door of the hospital. They left the car parked outside the main door, blue lights flashing, and ran in to the elevators and caught a closing door and hit the button for the fourth floor.

As the doors opened they pushed out and ran past the nurse's station to room 419 and found two hospital security guards, a nurse and an empty hospital bed.

"Where is he? Where's Peter Miller?" Eddie said, his breath heavy from running.

"We don't know," the nurse said. "I came down after you called and found his bed empty then called security. His chart says he was last checked on three hours ago."

"Shit," Eddie said. "Do you have security camera footage we can go through to see when he left and who he left with?"

"Sure thing," a short security guard said, his white uniform shirt at least a size too big for his small frame and his thick black leather belt hung loosely around his waist.

The guard called the security office while they were headed down to the basement level of the building and by they time they got there the video was queued up to what they were looking for, Dot Jeffries pushing Peter Miller out of his room in a wheelchair. The guard switched through footage from various cameras and tracked them to the elevator and down to the main lobby and right out the front entrance of the building to a black SUV.

"Can you make out the plates on the SUV?" Gus said.

"No sir, we don't have a good angle to read them," the guard said.

"We need to get to George and see what's going on," Eddie said.

GEORGE SILAS'S HOUSE was dark when they pulled into the driveway, not unusual for the middle of the night. Eddie rang the doorbell and knocked on the door while Gus tried to look through the glass to see if there was any motion.

"I'm going around back," Eddie said. "You wait here."

The side of the house was dark and Eddie moved slowly. He got to the back door and looked into the kitchen he had sat in just a few days ago drinking coffee with George and Gus.

Enough light came in through the back door window from a streetlight the block behind him for Eddie to see what he didn't want to see.

George Silas's body was face down on the kitchen floor.

Eddie stepped back and before thinking about it put his fist through the glass and reached in and unlocked the door, swung it open and hit the light switch and was at George's side within seconds. His fingers went to the man's throat and felt for a pulse.

"Eddie what the hell?" Gus came through the back door then saw George. "Is he alive?"

"There's a pulse but it's weak," Eddie said.

Gus had his Blackberry out and had 911 dialed and told the operator what they needed to know then called the Assistant Special Agent in Charge that they had an agent down.

CHAPTER 36

Eddie and Gus sat in the waiting room of the hospital while George Silas was taken through the ER, the side of his head indented from the heavy blow to his skull.

"We have George in the hospital," Eddie said. "And Dot on the run with Peter as a hostage."

"If she hasn't killed him by now," Gus said.

"If she hasn't killed him by now," Eddie said. "And a senator sitting in Washington, D.C. who needs to be behind bars."

"And don't forget an injured Aston Marshall on the loose," Gus said.

Eddie looked at Gus then jumped up and went to the check-in desk in the emergency room.

"Have you had a man come in within the last 24 hours with a bullet wound to the shoulder?" Eddie asked.

The man typed in the computer then turned back to Eddie.

"No, sir," he said. "But all gunshot wounds have to be reported to the police so you might check with them to see if any have been reported at other emergency rooms in the area."

"Thanks," Eddie said and went back to sit next to Gus.

"Probably smart enough not to go to a hospital," Gus said. "But I'll check anyway."

Gus called the Austin police department and went through two people before somebody finally had the information he was looking for then thanked them and hung up.

"A John Doe was brought in to St. David's four hours ago after being found passed out in a stolen van," Gus said.

"Gunshot wound?" Eddie said.

"To the right shoulder," Gus said. ".40 caliber."

"Has something finally gone right for us?" Eddie said.

"We'll see. He's sedated right now, but they have officers there due to the bullet wound and the stolen vehicle."

"With him out of commission then my sister and her family should be safe for now," Eddie said. "But let's leave them where they are just to be sure. Plus it's pissing off my brother-in-law more by the hour."

"Christmas is going to be fun for you," Gus said.

"Excuse me, Agent Ramirez," the man from the desk had walked over to him. "I just got word that George Silas has been admitted and is room 308."

The two men went up to the room and found their friend and boss in his hospital bed, his head elevated. Oxygen tubes ran into his nose and the left side of his face was bandaged. An IV ran from his arm and the liquid medicine slowly dripped from the bag into the clear line than ran to his bloodstream. His right eye was open.

"George," Gus said. "Can you hear me?"

"With one ear right now, as far as we can tell," Dr. Taylor walked in behind them then stopped when she realized it was Eddie and Gus.

"Does everyone you know get hit in the head?" she said to Gus.

"Eventually," Gus said.

She grinned at Gus and picked up George's chart.

"He'll need surgery to fix the shattered temporal bone but we needed to keep him stabilized at least overnight before that," she said. "It was a pretty good blow, but one inch one direction or the other and he wouldn't even be with us. His sinus cavities collapsed with the impact, protecting his brain. If he hadn't been brought in when he was the swelling in his skull would have killed him."

"I'll make sure he remembers that when reviews come up," Gus said.

"So Dr. Taylor," Eddie said. "I hope you've had a chance to catch up on your sleep."

"The two of you seem to be keeping the emergency room pretty busy," she said. "But yes, thank you, I was able to rest a bit."

Eddie reached in his pocket and pulled out a business card he'd had printed for his private detective services but hadn't handed out to anyone yet.

"Here," he said to her. "I know I came on a bit strong the other day, but perhaps I can make it up to you with dinner sometime."

"I appreciate that, Mr. Holland," she said. "I'll let you know."

"If the two of you are done can we talk to George?" Gus said.

"He needs rest," she said to the two of them. "Just keep it short."

Eva left the room and the men turned their attention back to George who was staring at Eddie with his one available eye.

"Don't…" George struggled to talk. "Don't mess with my doctor… until she's done with me."

"I won't, George," Eddie said, placing his hand on George's shoulder. "What can you tell us?"

"Chinese…two of them," George said. "Big guy with a .45 and a smaller guy."

He closed his eye and took a long breath through his nose.

"I was making…coffee," George said. "They knocked on the back door and pushed their way in when I opened it."

He rested before continuing.

"Said to call off the security on Dot and Peter. I told them I couldn't… The little one said, he knew… knew my wife was in Seattle, had someone watching her. That she'd be dead if I didn't."

"So you made the call?" Gus said.

"Wouldn't you?" George said, his eye closed. "He knew where she was, what she was eating."

"I would," Gus said.

"After I made the calls, the big guy...I just saw him pull the bat up to swing, then nothing until I woke up here."

"I'll get hold of your wife, make sure she's OK. And alert the Seattle field office and get her in protective care," Gus said.

"Thank you," George said. His eye closed for the last time for the night as he fell asleep.

CHAPTER 37

Eddie and Gus left the hospital and drove through downtown Austin contemplating their next move. Turning onto 6th Street the sidewalks were full of college kids and locals all there to enjoy the live music and liquid refreshments. Sounds of electric guitars, banjos, fiddles, and drums filled the air as they drove past each club.

"Where does the senator live?" Eddie said.

"I looked it up the other day," Gus said. "He has a big estate west of the city, just outside the Austin city line."

"Let's take a look," Eddie said.

Gus drove through downtown then wound through the smaller roads outside the city. After fifteen minutes of driving, he turned his headlights off and rolled to a stop. The only house in sight was on their left, well off the road. A row of lights lined each side of the long driveway that led to a circle in front of the large home, which had no lights on.

"Cozy," Eddie said.

"He was rich before running for office," Gus said. "His father was in oil and left it all to him. He sold most of the company, but rode the legacy. And being in office hasn't hurt either."

"How's that?" Eddie said.

"Of course knows about every bill that gets passed that benefits the oil and natural gas industry in the state and seems to always invest in the right companies at the right time, just as new funding is put in place that will help them grow."

"Insider trading?" Eddie said.

"Yup," Gus said. "But it's totally legal."

They watched the house a few minutes longer then Gus pulled away and turned his headlights on and circled back towards town. Eventually they ended up at the diner and ordered food and coffee and they sat staring out the window.

"I feel like we're at a boiling point," Eddie said. His eggs sat on their plate untouched and he'd only had three sips of his coffee.

"Agreed," Gus said. "There's not much else that could happen to aggravate the situation any more."

"Maybe it's time we do the aggravating," Eddie said.

"That is your specialty," Gus said.

AT THE FBI field office, Gus was at his computer and typing while Eddie sat at the next computer looking at aerial views of a home on the edge of the city with an online map. Gus hit the button to print out the request and retrieved it from the printer on the other side of the room. The two men walked it to the acting SAC's office when he arrived at 7:00am.

"What the hell is this?" SAC Hunter said.

"It's a search warrant," Gus said.

"I can see it's a search warrant but there's no judge in this city, or anywhere, that would sign this."

"That's fine," Gus said. "We just need it to get entered into the system."

Hunter looked at Gus as he thought about it then nodded.

"I get it," Hunter said. "Just watch yourselves."

"Understood," Gus said. The SAC signed the search warrant and Gus and Eddie walked it the six blocks to the courthouse to be submitted for a judge to sign. They watched as the clerk of the court typed the details of the warrant into the log for the state judicial system.

"You realize that…" the clerk said.

"Yes, I do," Gus said.

The clerk shook his head and continued typing. When finished he stamped the original document Gus had brought in and sent it on its way through the courthouse. Eddie and Gus walked outside into the morning heat.

"Ready to take a drive?" Eddie said.

"Might as well," Gus said. "Won't take long for this to go through the building."

They walked back to the field office and checked two pair of binoculars out from the supply clerk and grabbed two shotguns just in case. After retrieving Gus's cruiser from the underground parking garage they picked up sandwiches and coffee and headed west from downtown, passed Lake Travis, then turned onto a paved farm road.

CHAPTER 38

The black Charger sat idling on the side of a small road several miles outside of the city, as morning heat became early afternoon heat. Eddie and Gus kept their eyes trained on the sprawling home at the end of a long driveway with a row of black SUV's parked in the circle drive, inside the twelve foot tall security fence.

"How long do you think it will take?" Eddie said.

"I'm surprised it's taken this long," Gus said. "But it also depends on if they are here or not. We could be way off on this one."

"But if we're right," Eddie said, "as soon as word gets to them that we've requested a search warrant for the senator's house, they'll have to move Dot and Peter somewhere else."

"That's if they're still, well…" Gus said.

"I know, trust me, I know," Eddie said. "Let's hope Gerry Howard is the only casualty before this thing ends."

The loud ring of a cell phone broke the stillness of the car. Eddie reached into his jean's pocket and pulled out the disposable phone.

"Blocked number," Eddie said, looking at the screen. "Guess the word has spread." He opened the phone and hit the button to answer on speakerphone.

"Hello?"

"Special Agent Holland," Martin's voice came through the speaker, sounding tired. "Or former Special Agent Holland, I should say, I believe it's time we meet in person again."

"I'm a bit busy for a flight to D.C." Eddie said.

"Oh, I understand. Anyway, I'm already in Texas."

"You really didn't need to come all this way," Eddie said. "We were planning on having someone visit you to take you on a little tour of the Hoover building very soon."

"As fun as that would be, Mr. Holland, I think I'll pass," the senator said. "But I must congratulate you on your clever little game."

"Game?" Eddie said.

"Come now, Agent Holland," Martin said. "The search warrant was a cute idea. No judge in the state would sign a warrant to search a senator's house and you knew that."

"It was worth a shot, Mr. Barnett," Eddie said.

"And about meeting in person again, Mr. Holland," the senator said, "and I'm so looking forward to meeting your partner Agent Ramirez."

"Name the time and place, senator," Eddie said. "We'll be there."

"Oh, you already are. Perhaps you two old friends should take a look behind you," the senator said.

Eddie and Gus looked at each other then turned around in the car.

The rear window shattered as a white farm truck slammed into their trunk at more than forty miles an hour. Airbags inflated and deflated, throwing the two men's heads backwards then forwards and adding to the confusion.

Six men jumped out of a pair of black SUV's that had come in behind the truck and ran up on either side of the Charger. Black metal police batons shattered the windows. Another swing of the sticks and both men were unconscious in the mangled car.

CHAPTER 39

Eddie regained consciousness, hanging forward off a steel pole by his hands, which were bound together behind him and to the pole. His eyes opened slowly to see a pool of his own blood on the floor then saw a drip fall from beside his left eye into the deep red puddle. He saw his feet tied together and to the base of the pole with rope that was stained dark with blood that had run down his legs.

He stayed motionless to listen to the room before alerting anybody he was conscious. From behind him came a loud, strained breathing. Slowly he raised his head a few inches and scanned the room with his eyes, when he saw nothing he turned his head to his left to see the base of a wooden stairway going up to a door fifteen feet above.

To his right he saw Gus, tied to a matching pole but his body limp. He had slid down the pole, his knees on the hard cement and his bound hands and feet only six inches apart behind him on the pole.

Rotating as much as he could he saw the source of the strained breathing coming from behind him. Peter Miller sat tied to a wheelchair. His skin was grey. An IV line ran from his arm and the other end rested on the floor with no bag of vital fluids attached.

The sound of metal on metal, a key entering a keyhole, came from above as someone prepared to open the door at the top of the wooden stairs. Eddie hung his head low again and tried to relax to appear still unconscious as the footsteps of several people came down into the basement where he was being held.

"Mr. Holland," the thick Texas drawl of the senator filled the room. "No need for the dramatics; we have cameras."

Eddie raised his head to see Senator Barnett in the front of a group of Chinese men. He wore a seersucker suit and cowboy boots. Three of the others wore all black and the diminutive Mr. Xiao donned his usual black suit with a white shirt and a purple tie.

"I can only guess you have teamed up to cover your tracks," Eddie said. "With the three of us dead and Gerry Howard already gone nobody knows about your little act of treason."

"You are very wise, Agent," the senator said. "Once we established your true identity after your visit to D.C., we knew it was time to get out while we are ahead. And with this little mess cleaned up, I have time for my other endeavors."

"Such as?" Eddie said.

"Let's just say I feel drawn to serving not only the people of Texas, but of the United States as well," the senator said.

Eddie laughed out loud and leaned his head back to look the senator in the face.

"You think with all the skeletons in your closet you'll ever get close to the Oval Office?"

"What you see as skeletons, I see as votes," the senator said. "I will have given the orders to break up the largest case of espionage ever to take place on American soil. That alone will propel me to the front of the field. Anyway, I don't necessarily feel the need for all of that added pressure of the White House. I'll be quite content as Vice President."

"To stay right there in the Senate where you've been for years but with tie-breaking power," Eddie said.

"I am so pleased you understand how our government works, Mr. Holland," the senator said.

"You commit treason then expect to use that act as a way to get elected," Eddie said. "And I guess your Chinese friends will just sit back and let you tell the world everything that happened?"

"Yes, but with a few facts altered, of course," the senator said. "At this moment the CIA has a high ranking member of the Chinese intelligence department detained at an undisclosed location. Turns out he was working directly with Gerry Howard and Peter Miller to buy American military secrets."

"But he actually knew nothing about any of it so your name will never leave his lips in interrogation," Eddie said.

"You are far smarter than you look," the senator said.

"So, if Peter, Gus and I are just going to be killed, why are we tied up in this basement?" Eddie said.

"Only because you delivered yourselves to us by coming out to my estate," the senator said. "Our plan was for you and Agent Ramirez to die in an automobile accident. Mr. Miller was to be found after having committed suicide, tormented by the acts he committed against his country."

"What about Dot?" Eddie said.

"Ahh, yes, Ms. Jeffries," the senator said. "We debated about her and decided she could be a great help."

"So you told her that Peter had killed Gerry Howard, who was her uncle," Eddie said.

The senator looked down at Eddie and slowly raised his hands and quietly clapped them together several times.

"Bravo, bravo," the senator said. "I truly did not believe you had that piece of information."

"As you said, smarter than I look," Eddie said.

"Indeed," the senator said. "The late Mr. Howard raised Dot as his own after her own parents died in a car crash when she was only eight years old. Such a tragic story, don't you think? She was an invaluable assistant in removing Mr. Miller from the hospital."

"Plus she ruined your plan by shooting Peter in the shoulder," Eddie said. "Not really the optimal choice for a faked suicide injury."

"Correct again," the senator said. "But sadly, her usefulness will die, well, with you. Once you figured out, and likely reported to your supervisors, that Peter Miller killed Gerry Howard it was obvious that Dot would try again to avenge her uncle's death, but with more success. She will then take her own life. As for you and Agent Ramirez, we now we must resort to a more extreme solution."

"And what's that," Eddie said.

"It will all be on the 10:00 news tonight, but you won't be around to see it. Turns out two FBI agents broke into a senator's home without a search warrant hoping to find evidence of illegal activity."

"And they were shot by security guards," Eddie said.

"It was a bold move," the senator said. "They came in through a window in the basement. Security rushed down the stairs and a horrific shootout followed, ending in the death of the two trespassers and two security guards."

The senator pointed to the top of the stairs and traced the route security would take.

"Two security guards?" Eddie said. "How will you-"

The Chinese man in the purple tie stepped forward carrying Eddie's Glock 23 with his black leather gloved hand. He then turned and raised the gun and shot two of the three Chinese security guards in the head. The men fell were they were, taken off guard by their leader's actions. The limp body of one guard lay over the back of the other, single trails of blood coming from their foreheads.

"Oh," Eddie said. "Those security guards."

"Killed in the line of duty," the senator said, looking over at the two bodies, no sign of remorse. "An honorable death."

"I'm sure that will be very comforting to their families," Eddie said. "You don't get out to the movies very often, do you senator?"

"Not a fan, I must say," the senator said. "All that make believe is boring when real life is so exciting. Don't you think?" He raised his hands in the air and motioned around the room, looking at the bodies on the floor, the remaining Chinese guards and Peter Miller.

"Perhaps, but there's one thing you might have learned if you'd taken in a few more films in your time," Eddie said. "Especially ones involving evil villains, such as yourself."

"Honored," the senator said, holding his hand to his heart. "But what is that?"

"Well it seems that evil villains, such as yourself, always tend to talk too much," Eddie said. "In order to be a successful evil villain it turns out you have to be quite narcissistic and love to hear yourself talk."

"Perhaps I just felt you deserved the honor of knowing how we got to here and, more importantly, what will transpire after your demise," the senator said.

"That is much appreciated," Eddie said. "But there are some details that you don't yet know."

Eddie paused for effect and to try to buy more time as he tried to think of any way possible out of this. He looked over at Gus then twisted around to see Peter Miller then swung back around and lifted his head to the senator and the Chinese men.

"I believe the man with my gun there and the big guy behind him are the two who went to George Silas's home to get him to drop security on Dot and Peter," Eddie said.

"You are correct, but that is nothing I did not already know," the senator said.

"For some reason they did not complete their job and he is recovering in the hospital as we speak," Eddie said.

The senator turned to the man in the purple tie.

"Mr. Xiao," the senator said. "You told me that he was dead."

"An oversight," Mr. Xiao said. "He will be dead before tonight."

"Easier said than done," Eddie said. "He has more security on him than the President. Plus, he's already filed a full report and briefed his department on everything we've told him."

"We have friends in high places," the senator said. "Nothing will come of that. By now they will all have been ordered to stand down."

Eddie lowered and shook his head then rose back up to look at the senator.

"The entire Austin field office knows where we were this morning," Eddie said.

"Excellent," the senator said. "I won't have to tell as many stories to convince them why you were here."

"You may have trouble explaining the audio from our conversation in your office in D.C.," Eddie said. "While I convinced you to turn off your tape recorder I was taping the entire conversation."

The senator stared at Eddie as he thought back to the conversation and how much information he had divulged to the man he thought at the time to be Peter Miller.

"That is an illegally recorded conversation by a former FBI agent acting undercover without the sanction of the bureau," the senator said. "It will be thrown out of court before it's ever heard."

"What about the recording of this conversation?" Eddie said.

"What do you mean?" the senator said.

"Gus here likes gadgets," Eddie said. "When I gave him that digital recorder back he never returned it to the field office. It's strapped to his ankle under his sock right now, recording everything you've said."

Mr. Xiao motioned to his large counterpart who then stepped from behind him and over to Gus where he hung from the pole by his ankles and wrists. The ropes binding his feet kept him from getting to Gus's socks and a large knife was produced from his pocked and cut the ropes, letting Gus fall to his right onto the floor. He pulled both of Gus's shoes and socks off and turned to Mr. Xiao and the senator and shook his head.

While his head was turned away, Gus reached up and pulled the Heckler & Koch HK45 pistol from the guard's unsnapped holster. The guard felt the movement and reached for his holster and he turned back around to see the barrel of his own gun inches from his face. His left hand came up to push the gun aside as Gus pulled the firm trigger, the .45 caliber round at close range causing the man's face to explode in front of him.

Mr. Xiao had Eddie's gun out again and raised it to shoot Gus as the sound of a gunshot echoed through the room. Mr. Xiao fell to his knees, blood coming from his chest as a second shot struck him in the head.

Eddie looked to the top of the stairs to see Dot holding a black pistol, arms still extended out in front of her with the sights pointed at the man who was dying on the floor of the basement.

The senator began to reach inside his jacket.

"I would think twice before doing that, senator," Eddie said. The senator's hand moved back to his side.

Gus climbed to his feet, weak from his wounds and the struggle for the gun, and stepped to the senator and pulled a chrome Colt revolver from a brown leather holster under the senator's white jacket.

"Were you going to shoot us or blind us with the reflection off that thing?" Eddie said.

Dot ran down the stairs, grabbed the knife used to free Gus and cut the rope holding Eddie in place. He stood and took the black pistol from her then recovered his own Glock from the dead Chinese man. Dot ran to Peter and fell to her knees beside him.

"He's still alive!" Dot said.

"Is there anyone else upstairs?" Gus said.

"There was one guard watching me while I watched TV," Dot said. "I hit him over the head with vase."

"Ming?" Eddie said.

"What?" Dot said.

"Never mind." Eddie said.

CHAPTER 40

Eddie sat in a recliner in his sister's living room while Gus was resting on the sofa. The television was on the local news.

"Details are slow to emerge from the both the FBI and the Senator Barnett's office after the events of yesterday morning," a female reporter said, standing outside the black gate of the building Eddie and Gus had been tied up in a day earlier. "Unconfirmed reports say two FBI agents were inside this house when a shooting occurred."

"Senator Martin Barnett of Texas was seen being escorted out of his home in a black SUV," she said. "The FBI confirms the senator has been arrested and charged with attempted murder. More charges are expected to come. Three men were shot and have died and one woman has been taken into custody."

They sat quietly as the news show turned to sports then eventually to a commercial.

"What's going to happen to Dot?" Eddie said.

"She shot Peter so there's no getting around jail time," Gus said. "But she also helped to rescue us so that's being taken into consideration. There's talk of a minimum security prison sentence where Peter can visit regularly."

"She shoots him and he forgives her," Eddie said. "Amazing."

"I guess it's true love," Gus said.

The commercials ended and a puff piece about a horse and a dog that became best friends begins the next segment.

"So, I haven't asked yet," Gus said. "How did you know I was conscious?"

"What?" Eddie said.

"You obviously wanted the guard to come untie me to look for the recorder that wasn't even there," Gus said.

"Oh, that," Eddie said. "I had no idea you were conscious, wasn't even sure if you were alive. I was just trying to buy some time."

Gus stared at Eddie across the room.

CHAPTER 41

The building was a muted yellow brick with a dark brown wooden trim on the outside and the color scheme continued throughout the interior. Eddie walked slowly through the hallway, glancing cautiously through each open door. Most of the beds were empty and unmade, the room's occupants sitting in common areas staring at televisions, the floor, or nothing at all. It's how time was spent and it was what bothered Eddie the most: the waiting to die.

He stopped at room 218 before getting to where he could see in. The door was propped open by the grey metal stopper attached to the bottom of the thick slab of wood. Eddie knew he'd be there since he never left his room. Dinner was brought to him and most of the time fed to him when he refused to do it himself or he just ignored the fact that it was there.

Stepping around the corner into the small room Eddie heard the hissing sound of the oxygen tank in the corner, the mask laying on the bed unused. His father sat in a wheelchair facing the one window but his eyes focused on nothing in particular in front of him. Eddie went to the oxygen tank and turned the handle until it stopped hissing.

"Dad, you're going to kill yourself leaving this thing on," Eddie said.

His father sat there still looking at nothing.

Eddie pulled a chair with wooden arms and a pastel cloth seat over to the wheelchair and sat beside the old man.

"How've you been, Dad?" Eddie said.

He didn't expect a response and didn't receive one.

"Sorry it's been a while since I came to see you," Eddie said. "I've been busy with work."

The two men of two generations sat beside each other looking at and through the window over the back parking lot of the nursing home. Eddie thought of his childhood and his father and wondered what, if anything, his father thought about sitting here every day.

Eddie turned at a noise behind him as a nurse came in with the ever-present little white paper cup of pills and clear plastic cup of water.

"Mr. Holland," the nurse said. "It's time for your medicine."

Eddie noticed the slightest twitch of his father's face. The nurse stepped beside the older man and poured the pills from the cup into his mouth and his father leaned his head back to accept them, an automatic response to a repetitive process. He swallowed the water and the pills traveled down his throat to his stomach and his eyes returned to looking at the window.

"He usually has a few good minutes when those kick in," the nurse said.

"Thanks," Eddie said. "That would be nice."

They sat in the quiet room, ambient sounds of voices, carts being rolled and telephones from the hallway behind them.

"I left the FBI," Eddie said, "At least for a while."

He looked over at his father's face then back to the window as he watched a heavy-set nurse whose shift just ended getting into her car down in the parking lot.

"The politics of fighting crime takes more time than actually fighting crime," Eddie said. "And in anti-terrorism there were half a dozen agencies that never agreed on anything so nothing got done."

He thought he saw his father's hand move.

"So I'm working for myself, some investigation and detective work," Eddie said. "It feels good, better than it's felt in a long time. Like I'm making a small difference."

Eddie didn't know what else to say or what was getting through. They sat silently again as the afternoon sun moved and began casting longer shadows across the parking lot.

"I should be going," Eddie said. "I have a date tonight."

He stood and moved his chair back to the corner of the room then knelt down beside the wheelchair and put his hand on top of his father's hand, the old, rough skin felt alien to him.

"I'll try to come again soon," Eddie said.

His father's head slowly turned toward him and Eddie thought he saw his mouth move into a faint smile while they looked into each other's eyes for a few moments. The old man then turned his gaze back to the window and he was gone, trapped inside his own mind again. Eddie waited to see if there was any more to come, if his dad would come through the shell that had been left of him. He hoped, he longed, for a sentence, a word, or a sound. But none came.

Eddie leaned forward and kissed his father's forehead and turned to leave the room and stopped to look at the shelves around the old cathode ray tube television across from the hospital bed. A framed photograph of Eddie graduating the FBI Academy at Quantico stood next to one of Shelley with her husband and children. Beside that was a grainy photograph of his Dad standing in front of a helicopter, wearing army fatigues and helmet and holding a rifle to his side. The star emblem and designation of the Army Rangers 2nd Battalion was still visible on his sleeve.

He looked back at his dad then left the nursing home.

CHAPTER 42

Eddie pulled up at the address, a modern house painted bright red in a row of other modern houses painted primary colors about five miles from downtown. He rang the bell at exactly eight o'clock.

"Well, Eddie, punctual is a good start," Dr. Eva Taylor said after opening the door. Her hair was loose this time and flowed past her neckline and down her back. She appeared to be wearing no makeup and wore perfectly fitting jeans and a white blouse through which Eddie could see her silhouette while she was backlit in the doorframe. He wondered momentarily if she knew this and decided she did.

"Punctuality is probably my best quality," Eddie said. "And I wanted to thank you again for calling."

"It was more out of pity than anything else," she said with a smile.

"I would ask if you were ready to go but it's obvious you are. You look amazing," Eddie said.

"Why, thank you," she said, putting one hand on her hip with a little pose.

"You feeling fun or fancy?" Eddie said.

"Fun," Eva said. "Always fun."

THEY SAT ACROSS from each other at a corner table at the Hyde Park Grill as they sipped on the last glasses from a bottle of a Willamette Valley Pinot Noir Eddie had ordered for them, their dinner plates already cleared away.

"Are you often in situations where you might get hit in the head, or was your hospital visit that day a chance encounter?" Eva said.

"It unfortunately does come up occasionally in my line of work, though I honestly end up on the winning side most often."

"Your friend, Gus, with the shiny badge, do you work with him?"

"That's kind of a long story that ends with a 'yes and no'," Eddie said. "I'm currently on a leave of absence from the bureau."

"Oh. Was this your choice or theirs?"

"Blunt, I like it," Eddie said. "Mine. I just needed some time away."

"It sure looks like you're getting time away," she said, his face still bruised from the activities a week earlier.

"Well, that was my intention. Just to distract myself from having nothing to do I've been taking small jobs from the law firm where my sister works. Usually cheating husbands and child support types of things. And that's actually how this happened," he motioned to his face.

"Why did you need time away from the FBI?" she said.

Eddie sat and thought before answering, not having given a direct answer to the direct question since taking the leave.

"Gus and I grew up together here in Austin, went to college together, and were both accepted into the FBI. We graduated Quantico and Gus was sent to St. Louis," Eddie said. "I was sent to D.C. That was spring of 2001."

"Oh," Eva said.

"In the course of a year the FBI went from being an organized crime and financial crimes culture to a leading force in anti-terrorism. Many of the senior agents weren't prepared for that kind of change, so it was the young guys that picked up the pieces."

"And you were right in the middle of it all," Eva said.

"I spent the next ten years tracking down sleeper cells, following every lead about foreign and domestic terror threats and always wondering if I missed anything that would lead to the death of more people."

"Sounds... stressful," Eva said.

"I watched a lot of great agents get divorces, become alcoholics or simply burn out and fade away," Eddie said. "I felt I was on that path last year, so I decided to try to keep it from happening."

"And?" Eva said.

"So far, so good," Eddie said. "Though that fight will never end, it's just the nature of our world now, I don't think that's what I'll go back to. It's time again for the young guys to pick up the pieces and lead the way."

Eddie swallowed the last of his wine and they looked at each other over the candle that had burned its way down to a pool of liquid wax, the wick floated freely with just an ember of light left of the flame that had burned for the last hour.

Eddie drove Eva home and they sat in his car and talked and laughed, then they sat in his car and kissed. He eventually walked her to the front door.

"Would you like to come in?" Eva said, taking a momentary pause from kissing him to speak.

"I would, you see," Eddie said. "But I'm not a slut."

"Hey!" Eva punched his chest.

"I would like nothing more than to spend the night with you," Eddie said. "But I would rather wait and spend a lot more nights with you."

Eva ran her hands down either side of Eddie's face and reached up and kissed him one last time, then smiled at him and went inside and closed the door behind her.

After staring at the closed door and immediately regretting his decision, Eddie walked to his car and turned the ignition on. He pressed the button on the CD player to turn it on and Charlie Sexton's voice, somehow smooth and gravelly at the same time, filled the small car.

With the shifter in first gear, Eddie pulled his foot off the clutch and began to roll forward when the cell phone in his pocket vibrated. He pushed the clutch back in and put the brake on and pulled the phone out and read the small display:

'In case you change your mind, the door is unlocked.'

He stared at the display then put the phone back in his pocket, turned the car off and walked as casually as possible back to the house and turned the unlocked handle of the front door. The house was quiet and mostly dark, a small glow of light coming down the stairs from the second level.

He took off his brown plaid fedora and tossed it on the dining room table and folded his hounds tooth sports coat over the back of a chair. Slowly walking up the stairs he heard movement upstairs and followed the sounds to the door of Eva's bedroom, open only a few inches.

Eddie pushed the door open and stepped into the bedroom.

"Eva," he said. The bathroom light was on across the room and the water was running in the shower. Eddie's heart began to beat heavier.

He walked around the queen-sized bed to the bathroom door and looked into the small, bright room. Eva was in the shower, dressed and slumped on the floor and unconscious.

Eddie froze and stopped breathing as he listened quickly then turned around to see Aston Marshall step out from behind the bedroom door, a black leather sap in his right hand.

"You got me once with that thing, it isn't going to happen again," Eddie said.

"We'll see about that," Aston Marshall said.

Still standing in the bathroom doorway Eddie hit the light switch, killing the only source of light in the room, then dove forward into a roll, coming up just left of where the man was now standing. From the kneeling position he'd ended up in, Eddie's right hand came up and he struck Aston in the chest with his palm just as he was turning on the bedroom light. Marshall fell backward into the wall then recovered and raised the sap to his side and swung and Eddie's head at his waist level.

Eddie leaned back out of the way of the swing, feeling the rush of air from the lead ball filled leather sap barely miss his face then caught Aston's swinging right hand with his own as his left came up and struck the elbow with full force, the crack of the man's radial bone easily heard and felt, then brought his fist down onto his right shoulder where he had been shot a week earlier.

Aston Marshall stumbled forward, the sap falling to the floor as he grabbed at his broken bone and turned to see Eddie closing the distance again. Aston swung with his left arm, barely landing a wincing blow on Eddie's right cheek, as Eddie stuck his left foot firmly on the carpet and spun to bring his right foot around and extended his leg out, landing the kick into the stomach of his taller opponent.

Still on his feet, Aston stood doubled over, winded from the kick and in pain from the broken arm. Eddie grabbed Aston's graying hair and forced him to stand up straight.

"You done?" Eddie said.

With his good arm Aston grabbed Eddie's left hand from the top of his head, stretched the arm out as he rotated away and went into almost a kneeling position then pulled the arm down on his shoulder as he stood quickly. Turning left again, he brought his elbow back hard into Eddie's ribs, cracking two.

Eddie fell forward, the pain from his side restricting his breathing, as Aston stumbled and the movement causing the broken bone in his arm to move and push at his stretched skin from the inside. Slowly the two men stood and turned to face each other again, Eddie's left arm clutched to his ribs and Aston's right arm hanging useless to his side.

After assessing each other, Aston began to charge at Eddie, counting on his height and weight advantage to overtake him.

"Eddie!" Eva said, leaning on the doorframe to the bathroom.

Aston hesitated and turned towards the woman's voice as Eddie stepped in and landed a punch to the side of Aston's face as he was turning back towards him.

Aston fell to his knees and clutched his face as blood came from between his fingers from the broken nose and the front tooth that had been knocked out and was loose inside his mouth. Eddie stood over him and Aston looked up and spit the tooth up at him. With his right hand Eddie once again grabbed Aston's hair and smashed his already mangled face against his knee and the man fell to the floor.

Eddie stepped over the unconscious body to Eva. She collapsed forward into him. He winced with pain and held her tightly then sat her on the edge of the bed and picked up the handset to the phone on her nightstand and dialed 911.

"This is Special Agent Eddie Holland with the FBI," Eddie said to the emergency operator. "I need police and ambulance to my location immediately."

"Yes, sir. We have your address from the caller ID and are dispatching now," the operator's voice came across the line. "Do you want me to alert the FBI field office?"

"No, I'll handle that," Eddie said and hung up the phone. He dialed Gus's number and told him the address and a quick assessment of the situation then sat beside Eva and she put her arms around him and held him until the ambulance arrived.

CHAPTER 43

Eddie and Gus sat in a booth at the diner. Their meals eaten and plates cleared, two cups of coffee in front of them.

"Aston Marshall was in county lock-up while waiting on transfer to a federal facility," Gus said. "When a nurse came to change the dressing on his bullet wound in the infirmary he knocked her out, killed a guard and took his gun and escaped. He followed you from your apartment to Eva's house, then waited for you to return."

"Why even bother?" Eddie said. "The senator is in custody."

"He didn't know that," Gus said. "And I guess he has a strong work ethic, committed to finishing the job."

They sat and drank their coffee.

"How's Eva?" Gus said.

Eddie sat his coffee down and stared at the dark liquid.

"That woman," he said, "is unlike any I've ever met. She's back at work today."

"Seriously?" Gus said.

"Yeah. She told me she understands the nature of my job, of our job, and that sometimes the line between work life and personal life is crossed."

"Amazing," Gus said. "You gonna see her again."

"Maybe," Eddie said and grinned.

"Oh, yeah. I got you something," Gus said. He reached into his briefcase on the seat beside him and placed a small box on the table in front of Eddie.

"You shouldn't have," Eddie said.

"You'll really be saying that in a minute," Gus said.

Eddie picked up the box and pulled the top off and looked inside.

"Between you and my sister, I guess there's no way I can't take this," Eddie said.

He pulled the phone out of the box, the smooth glass touch screen still covered with protective plastic.

"It's the new standard issue phone for the FBI," Gus said. "You're the first in the office to get one."

"But I'm not active duty," Eddie said.

"Well, you see, it's like this," Gus said. "George has decided to take early retirement to spend time with his wife so she never has to travel without him again."

"Oh?" Eddie said.

"And the new SAC insisted that we get you a cell phone or else," Gus said. "Seems he had the crazy idea of making you a special consultant to the Austin field office, at least until you decide to come back full time."

"Wow," Eddie said. "And who is the new SAC?"

Gus smiled at Eddie and Eddie grinned.

Eddie pressed the button on the phone until it was turned on and a photo of Gus's face appeared on the screen.

"Nice touch," Eddie said.

"Thought you'd like that," Gus said.

CHAPTER 44

The rain began and soaked the damaged earth. The brown grass returned, if only momentarily, to being green and the trees seemed to stretch their branches wide to collect as much of the water as they could. High school football played on in downpours and the fans filled the stands. Children walked to school with brightly colored raincoats and jumped in puddles along the way.

Eddie ran shirtless, letting the rain run through his hair and down his face and into his eyes. His ribs were healed but still sore, slowing his pace but not stopping him. His face no longer showed the signs of the fight with Aston Marshall or the abuse in the senator's basement.

He rounded the corner to his street then slowed and walked through the courtyard, which now showed signs of life from the liquid sustenance. He climbed the stairs and opened the unlocked door to his apartment. His shoes came off and he hung them upside down on the back of a chair to dry out. Walking to the bathroom he removed his shorts and opened the swinging glass door to his shower, the water was already running and steam flooded out.

"You're awake," Eddie said.

Eva smiled and stepped over to let Eddie into the small shower with her and he pulled the door closed behind him.

"You know I have a walk-in shower with two nozzles and a built in bench at my house," Eva said.

"Your point?"

"That bench could come in handy."

She reached her arms around him, pressing her body into his and ran her soapy sponge across his back.

CPSIA information can be obtained
at www.ICGtesting.com
Printed in the USA
LVHW031940090120
643080LV00007B/1112/P